SHE LAY BOUND AND GAGGED IN THE BEDROOM CLOSET.

Her throat had been cut almost to the spinal column. Her eyes were wide open and a piece of tissue paper, part of the gag that had been crammed all the way to her windpipe, dangled from the left side of her mouth.

The delicately etched face had been hideously contorted by pain. Yet it seemed to retain the features of a small child.

"A novel of beauty and power. BLOOD INNOCENTS is a remarkably 'real' novel filled with flesh-and-blood characters and vivid prose."
—Thomas Gifford,
author of THE WIND CHILL FACTOR

Blood Innocents

Thomas H. Cook

BERKLEY BOOKS, NEW YORK

This Berkley book contains the complete
text of the original edition.

BLOOD INNOCENTS

A Berkley Book / published by arrangement with
the author

PRINTING HISTORY
Playboy Press edition / April 1980
Berkley edition / September 1986

ISBN: 0-425-09358-1

For Susan Terner

Rachmonus

His humanism is therefore restricted to the contemplation of isolated individuals in contemporary society. Now, this society is itself only a form of the alienation that has got to be transcended.

————Henri Lefebvre, *Dialectical Materialism*

At the beginning of everything there is first of all refusal.

————Jean-Paul Sartre

1

MONDAY

Watching it from his window, Reardon saw the city
only as an immense patchwork of random sound and
directionless movement. It had not always been like
this for him. In his youth he had walked the streets
in his dark-blue uniform with shining badge as a protector of a wild and famous city. He had not forgotten
that what he felt then was a rapture so heedless, asking
so little, that even the loss and butchery he saw in the
course of his duties could not permanently overwhelm
it. He had been a serious protector, one who must love
what he protects.

He lit a cigarette. The flame gave off a pale,
orange aurora in the morning fog. He watched the
match burn down almost to his fingertips, then quickly
waved it out. He smoked wearily, pleasurelessly. This
would be his last cigarette, and because of that he
could not savor it. In his mid-fifties now, he had come
to fear the slow, strangulating death of lung cancer.

It was cancer that had finally killed his wife, Millie,
slowly devouring her bowels inch by inch. Even now,
two weeks after her funeral, he sometimes came home
to the apartment expecting to find her there and was
forced all over again to relive his loss of her. At the
funeral he had sat at the front of the church staring
at the roses that had adorned her closed coffin. He

had ordered her coffin closed because he believed that death was a kind of final privacy, upon which living eyes should not be allowed to intrude. His son, Timothy, had sat beside him, along with his son's wife, Abbey, and their children. Timothy had kept his hands folded ritually in his lap, his face immobile, but with his eyes darting about as if his mind were still busily examining the law cases in his office. And Reardon had noticed that only when his son looked back over his shoulder and saw the head of his law firm enter the church did his face suddenly change its expression to one of mourning.

Now, standing in his living room, Reardon turned from the window and glimpsed himself in the full-length mirror on the opposite side of the room. He had become much more conscious of his body recently, conscious that it was slowly taking him through that process of things that pass away. He was still powerfully built for a man of ordinary height and weight, but now, staring at himself across the room, he could detect the first curving downward of his shoulders and buckling of his knees.

Quickly he turned from the mirror to the window. Below he could hear the traffic cutting through the wet streets like long knives slicing into melons. He remembered a psychopath he had arrested almost twenty years before. When asked why he had butchered his victim so wantonly the man had replied he was looking for seeds. "You know, like in a watermelon."

Reardon tapped his cigarette and watched the ashes tumble toward the street. He estimated the distance from his window to the street at about eighty feet. He had heard of infants surviving falls of even more than that distance, but never an adult. Babies survived because they relaxed all the way down. But adult human beings, terrified beyond comprehension, stiffened every muscle, locked every joint, stretched every tendon taut and ground their bones like sticks of chalk into the sidewalk.

Slowly his eyes followed upward the line of windows in the building facing him. He had answered many calls there, mostly inconsequential: family bickerings, lovers' quarrels, evictions, disorderly conduct complaints, general nuisance behavior; only once a murder. Finally his field of vision passed the highest landing and over the roof, where, in the distance, half blurred by the early morning fog, a sign blinked its certain message that Jesus Saves.

"Got a freako for you this morning, Reardon," Sergeant Smith said from behind his large wooden desk as Reardon entered the precinct house. For Smith human crime was divided into three categories: ordinary criminal acts—such as theft, simple battery, rape and common murder—for which no specific designation was required; "bloodies," which were particularly gruesome murders or assaults; and "freakos," crimes so bizarre that Smith could not comprehend their source.

"What is it?" Reardon asked.

"Piccolini will tell you," Smith said teasingly.

"You can tell me."

"No, let Piccolini. It's a little different, you know what I mean?" Smith winked at Reardon. "It's something they think only Detective Reardon can handle. Something they need an expert for." He motioned toward Piccolini's office door with a grand, mocking gesture. "You may enter, sir."

Piccolini sat at a gray metal desk. Each wall was lined with file cabinets and the window behind Piccolini featured a view of the rear alley. Piccolini's desk was covered with files, and he was furiously applying himself to a stack of papers in front of him when Reardon entered.

"Smith says you want to see me." Reardon said.

Piccolini did not look up. "Sit," he said.

Piccolini did everything with the single-minded purpose and intensity of a worker ant. Details were his passion. He believed that if a social security number was recorded incorrectly it could lead to general disorder. For Piccolini great upheavals were nothing more than the accumulated consequence of millions of small mistakes.

Reardon's eyes roamed Piccolini's office. It was a habit of his, looking for evidence even when there was no crime. A small metal bookshelf stood in a corner opposite the door. The books were arranged alphabetically by title. There were codes of conduct, commission reports, manuals of procedure and handbooks on administration: the rules of the game. Places were marked in some of them, Miranda warning cards used as bookmarkers.

"Want coffee?" Piccolini asked without looking up.

"No," Reardon said.

"Be through in a minute. Just relax. I have to get all this out every Monday morning."

Reardon did not know very much about Piccolini even though he had known him for years. He knew he was a devout Catholic who believed in an absolute fate, his own and everybody else's. This, Reardon believed, explained his generally acknowledged fearlessness. Otherwise Piccolini was an enigma. Reardon knew that he was married, but not whether he was happy in that marriage. He knew that he had children, but did not know if they loved their father. He knew that Piccolini drove an expensive car, but he did not know if it was paid for.

Piccolini finished signing the last paper and looked up at Reardon. "I suppose Smith told you we have a bloody for you this morning."

"He called it a freako," Reardon said.

"Where does he get those classifications?"

"I don't know."

"They always give me the creeps."

Reardon said nothing.

Piccolini leaned back in his swivel chair and put his hands behind his head. "Have you ever been to the Children's Zoo?"

"Sure," Reardon said.

"Well, you remember a few years back when Wallace Van Allen donated two fallow deer to the Zoo? It was in all the papers. It was a big event, you know? On television and all that."

"I remember it."

"Well, we have an embarrassing situation here," Piccolini said. "It has to do with those same deer."

"What about them?"

Piccolini cleared his throat and shifted slightly in his seat. From the earliest days of their association together Reardon had noticed that Piccolini was seldom unnerved by seeing the results of a crime or by the brutal details of investigating it, but that he did not like to describe a crime to others. Rendering it into language removed it from that remote spot it occupied in his mind. It was only in describing a crime that Piccolini seemed compelled by its reality.

"Somebody killed them," Piccolini said.

"The deer?"

"Yes."

"Shot them?"

Piccolini shook his head. "No," he said, "hacked them to death."

"Hacked them to death?" Reardon had never heard of such a thing.

"That's right," Piccolini said. "We think maybe some political types did it. You know, Wallace Van Allen is rich and famous and all that. Very visible, if you know what I mean. Prominent. Always on television doing something. Giving money to this organization, supporting that candidate. Big charity types. Social types too. Big Liberals."

"So you think it's a political angle? Political enemies of the Van Allens?"

"Nothing personal," Piccolini said, "nobody who actually knew Van Allen. But it still could have been radical types, some crazy, off-the-wall radical group maybe. You never know what they might do."

Reardon nodded. "And they killed a guard, I guess."

"No, just the deer."

"But I'm in homicide."

"Now look," Piccolini said, "this is a big case. One of the biggest. Some real big people are looking in on this one, interested in it, if you know what I mean. I know you're in homicide, but this is bigger than a homicide right now, and the people downtown want top people on it all the way." Piccolini smiled. "And that means you, John. You were recommended for this case, and you've got it. Solving it could be a big plus."

Reardon was fifty-six years old and a detective; he did not need any more big pluses and was surprised Piccolini could think he did. "I have some other cases to clear up first," he said.

"Forget them," Piccolini snapped. "As of right now this is your only case. It's the biggest case in this precinct, and it may be the biggest case in New York right now, and you're the chief investigating officer on it."

"But what about the other cases?"

"All your cases have been reassigned," Piccolini said. "You can take some time and brief the new guys, but after that, get on the deer. And get on it fast, will you, John? Believe me, the precinct is on the line in this one."

"Sure," Reardon said dully. He had heard that before. Everybody was on the line in every case.

"This one is for real," Piccolini said emphatically. "We need to break this one fast, real fast. So forget about homicide for a while and concentrate on collaring the guy who hacked those deer to death."

Reardon did not reply.

"Go out and see those deer," Piccolini said sentimentally. "You should see what that guy did to them. And they didn't even have horns to defend themselves with."

Reardon nodded but said nothing.

"Well, okay," Piccolini said, "that's it. Get on it."

"I'll keep you informed," Reardon said dryly.

"Yeah, I want a regular update on this one. I want to know the moment anything breaks."

"Sure," Reardon said.

"Good luck."

As he closed the door of the office behind him, Reardon could hear Piccolini returning ferociously to the papers on his desk. It sounded like a rat scrambling through dry leaves.

A number of detectives had already assembled around Reardon's desk in the homicide bullpen by the time he came out of Piccolini's office. As he seated himself behind his desk they mumbled their good mornings, then slouched casually against the desks that surrounded his. With the exception of Ben Whitlock, they were all younger men than he, leaner too and hungrier for advancement: New York's finest wolves. There was not one who might not someday be Chief of Detectives, and there was not one, except Whitlock, whom Reardon trusted. In their presence Reardon felt spectacularly out of place. Their youth aged him and their ambition tired him.

He pulled out a group of folders from a side drawer and laid them on top of his desk. "I guess Piccolini sent you here," he said.

"He said you'd fill us in on your cases," Larry Merchant said, "the ones we'll be handling while you're on the other thing."

"Right." Reardon pulled one of the folders from the stack and opened it. "I'll start with you first," he told Merchant, "but I want all of you to come in sometime and review all these cases, whether they're assigned to you or not, just in case you run across something that might be helpful."

He handed Merchant the folder. "This is the Alverez case. You can check the file for the details, but this is basically it. Maria Alverez was found beaten to death in her apartment on East 71st Street. She was a high-class hooker, not the Eighth Avenue variety. Her pimp was a man named Louis Fallachi. He has a few low-level syndicate connections, but nothing big, nothing fancy. Strictly a ham-and-eggs muscle man, a bone breaker for a few shylocks. We've checked him out closely, and there's no evidence as yet that he had anything to do with the killing. We've tried to reconstruct Alverez's movements the night she died. We know that she wasn't hooking that night. She went to a movie with a girlfriend. The doorman in her building says that she got home around eleven o'clock. So far he's the last person to have seen her alive. The next morning she was dead. We have the weapon, a plain carpenter's hammer. No prints."

"Any witnesses?" Merchant asked glumly.

"Not so far," Reardon said, "but this happened only a couple of days ago. The area is still being canvassed. Somebody might turn up who saw something. The main thing at this point is to find out everybody she knows and check them out. She may have known the person who did it, because he probably came through the front door, and there's no evidence of forcible entry."

"What'd she look like?" Merchant asked with a grin.

"What difference does it make?" Reardon said coldly.

Merchant shifted his body nervously to the left. "Just curious, that's all."

"There are pictures of her in the file," Reardon said.

"Right," Merchant said. "I'll get on it." He ducked out of the group and quickly marched upstairs to the file room.

Reardon did not know why he disliked Larry Merchant. He thought the reason might be the easy way Merchant took up his cases, as if they were just so many used cars he had to clear off the lot before the Saturday shipment of new ones, or the fact that he took his pay and ran off to the suburbs to spend it, leaving the city to wallow in its squalor like an old whore—used, abused, forgotten.

Reardon picked Charlie Darrow for the David Lowery case because David Lowery had been six years old when he was murdered, and Reardon knew that the killing of a child was a crime that shot Darrow up to a high adrenaline range. Darrow would be relentless in his pursuit, tireless, utterly oblivious to the distinction between being on duty and off duty.

"David Lowery was last seen alive by a few of his playmates in an alley off East 83rd Street," Reardon began. He handed Darrow the folder. "Three hours later his body was found stuffed in the trunk of an abandoned car on 122nd Street. He had been strangled with a jump rope and his body had been sexually abused."

Darrow's face hardened. "How old did you say he was?"

"Six years old. He was a small child for his age. Not quite three feet tall."

"Jesus Christ," Darrow said.

"The car had been sitting on 122nd Street for a few days," Reardon said. "The owner is a grocery store manager up in Yonkers. He reported the car stolen quite some time ago. He's being checked out. He seems to be clean."

Darrow nodded. "Nothing funny in his background?"

"Not that we've been able to uncover yet. Everything that we know about him is in the file. A few people in the neighborhood of 122nd Street saw a man and a boy around the car, but nobody saw the child's body put into it. There's also this: two days before the boy was killed the desk sergeant received an anonymous complaint about noisy kids playing in that same car in the afternoon. For now, that's it."

"Not much then," Darrow said disappointedly.

"Not much," Reardon agreed, "but there's never very much in the beginning."

"Sure," Darrow said, and walked away from Reardon's desk.

Reardon turned to Wallace Chesterton. "The next one's for you."

"All right," Chesterton said.

Wallace Chesterton was a large, ponderously built man with a fiery temper, a bully who had been formally disciplined several times. He believed that the best way to approach either a witness or a suspect was to assault him, sometimes verbally, sometimes physically. So Reardon gave Chesterton the closest thing he had to a routine gangland killing, because he knew it would probably never be solved. Chesterton would know that too and be less inclined to rough up somebody for nothing.

"This one is strictly by the book," Reardon told him. "A routine gangland rubout. Clean. The victim is a guy named Martin Scali. He was found in a parked car near the East River with one bullet through the back of his head. He had two hundred and thirty-eight dollars in his wallet. He has all kinds of gangland connections. As usual, no witnesses. Nobody heard or saw anything. You've got a guy with a bullet in his head and that's it."

Chesterton frowned. "Shit."

"Do the best you can." Reardon handed Chesterton the folder. "There's not much in it."

Chesterton shrugged. "Yeah," he said and stalked out toward the file room.

Reardon gave his last case of the morning to Ben Whitlock, who was neither young nor exceptionally competent but in whom Reardon continued to sense the old, special calling of the law. Whitlock was incorruptible. He had lived through one Police Department scandal after another and had always emerged untouched.

"I guess the last one's for you, Ben," Reardon said with a slight smile.

"Why are they pulling you off all these cases, John?" Whitlock asked.

"They're pulling me off more than these cases," Reardon said. "They're pulling me off all my cases."

"Why are they doing that?"

"Because they want me to handle that deer killing in the zoo. Over in Central Park."

"That's not a homicide." Whitlock looked at Reardon suspiciously. "What the fuck is all this about?"

"You mean why are those deer so important?"

"Yeah."

"Well, it's not the deer. It's who they belonged to."

"They were just in the zoo, right?"

"They were given to the zoo by Wallace Van Allen."

Whitlock nodded. "I get it," he said. "Yeah, that explains it. Some fat cat gets his deer killed, so everyone downtown goes into a panic."

"That's about it." Reardon admitted. He felt a stir of respect for Whitlock, his old colleague, who had triumphed for so long against internal politics and external corruption, like an old mastiff, guardian of the gate, who eats from no man's hand. "I'm sorry we didn't work together more all these years."

"Yeah, me too," Whitlock said, "but that's the way it is."

"Maybe we'll get a case together someday yet."

"Maybe. But not likely. They keep assigning me new partners every year or so. It's always been like that. Ever since I got my gold shield they've been jerking me off. Jerking me around from partner to partner."

"Yeah, I've noticed that."

"They've been trying to get rid of me for twenty years," Whitlock said wearily.

"Well, you're still here."

"Not for long," Whitlock said. "I think I'm gonna grab the option. Early retirement, you know? I think I'm ready to let go the line, you know what I mean?"

"You mean it?"

"Yeah, I'm tired. Whipped." Whitlock winked. "Who knows, maybe the wife and me can get to Florida. Somewhere south, out of this. Get some sun, you know, before the last sunset."

Reardon nodded. He did not know what to say. He knew only that he did not want to see Whitlock go. He had never gone to Whitlock for anything, but he had liked knowing Whitlock was there in case he came across something he could not handle alone.

"Well, what do you have for me?" Whitlock asked.

Reardon glanced down at his desk. "The victim's name is William Sebastian Falkner. He was murdered in the back of his dry cleaning shop last Thursday. Shot three times in the head and once in the chest with a .22-caliber pistol. The motive is presumed to be robbery, since all the money in the house and shop was taken."

Whitlock chuckled. "Yeah, that kind of forces you to presume robbery."

Reardon smiled. "A local teenager named Culverson was seen hanging around the shop not long before the murder. Culverson is a rough case. He's got a juvenile record that's pretty impressive, and he's been under suspicion for armed robbery in the past. His last address was three blocks from the shop. We're watching his apartment, but he hasn't turned up. The details are in the file." Reardon closed the folder and handed it to Whitlock. "That's about it."

"Okay," Whitlock said. "I'll check it."

"Good luck. If you need anything, let me know. I'll be around."

Whitlock started to walk away; he stopped at the door and turned back to Reardon. "Sorry to hear about Millie," he said.

Reardon had not thought about Millie for the past few moments, and suddenly hearing her name again thrust him back into a vague, aching gloom. "Thanks" was all he said.

"It happens to everybody," Whitlock said. "A vale of tears, you know?"

"Yeah," Reardon said. He watched Whitlock disappear up the stairs. So that was it, he thought—a bludgeoned prostitute, a strangled child, a dead gangland punk and a murdered shopkeeper.

And two slaughtered deer in the Children's Zoo.

The whole area around the cage of the fallow deer had been cordoned off by police roadblocks. But even in the chill, late autumn air a crowd had gathered, pressing against the roadblocks and craning their necks over the shoulders of the uniformed patrolmen assigned to keep them back. Another group of police was milling around outside the deer cage, and Reardon could not see inside the cage until they parted to let him pass.

In the cage each of the bodies had been covered by a black tarpaulin. Several rivulets of blood trickled out from beneath one of the tarpaulins and ran in jagged lines to the bars. When blood flowed like that, Reardon knew, it usually meant that many wounds had been inflicted. But the blood ran in one broad swath from beneath the other tarpaulin. That would mean that only one wound had been inflicted, and that it was deep and had brought death almost immediately.

Detective Mathesson was standing calmly between the two bodies of the fallow deer. He was a very large man, but the heavy black overcoat and gray hat made him appear even more massively built. His legs were spread wide apart like a gunslinger's and he was rubbing his gloved hands together vigorously for warmth. "Hello, John," he said as Reardon approached.

Reardon nodded.

"Only in New York," Mathesson said.

"What?"

"Look at it. Only in New York."

"Oh," Reardon said, "yeah."

"At least they're not people," Mathesson said, "that's one good thing."

Reardon looked down at the body to the left. Covered as it was, it did not look that different from the human bodies he had seen. It was small, crumpled, motionless and, above all, utterly silent.

"In a way I wish they were," Mathesson said.

Reardon squinted at him. "Why?"

"Because it would mean the killer's normal, in a way."

"What do you mean?"

"Well, if this had been done, say, to a couple of people, children or old people or women, then it wouldn't be that uncommon," Mathesson said. "We've dealt with that sort of thing before. We're used to it. It's not that weird. And we'd get the guy that did it. Probably pretty soon, too."

"Maybe," Reardon said. It was his favorite response to statements he found either ridiculous or inane.

"But this is real strange," Mathesson said, his eyes moving back and forth between the two covered bodies, "and it'll spread to people."

"You think so?"

"Sure it will," Mathesson said. "Doesn't it always?"

"Sometimes."

"Most of the time." Mathesson looked at Reardon. "Don't you remember that guy with the cats? That complaint we got about a guy giving cats baths in hydrochloric acid?"

"Yes," Reardon said quickly. He did not need to hear it again.

"Well, we collared him a couple of times for that, but you remember it didn't stop him. Nothing stopped him until he gave the same bath to a ten-year-old girl."

Reardon said nothing.

"That's the way it'll be with this case," Mathesson said. "Same thing. He won't stop with animals. He won't stop with these deer. Not if I know this guy. He's really weird, and that means he'll be hard to catch."

"Well, anyway, let's get on it," Reardon said wearily. "We have to catch him sometime."

"Sure." Mathesson nodded toward the covered bodies. "You want to see them?"

"Yes," Reardon said.

Mathesson lit a cigarette and walked over to one body. "This is the worst one." With one quick gesture he jerked the covering from the body of the fallow deer.

Reardon was jolted by what he saw. The head had been reduced to a pulpy mass. The partition between the nostrils had been severed with one clean blow. One eyeball had been gouged from the head and now dangled by its distended muscles between the socket and the upper jaw. The neck and upper torso were such a patchwork of cuts and bruises that it would have been difficult to tell the color of the deer without looking at its hindquarters. Both front legs were broken and one was almost severed at the knee joint.

Suddenly Reardon was seized by an almost uncontrollable sadness. He stepped back from the body and took a deep breath to stop the shuddering sensation in his chest.

"You all right?" Mathesson asked.

Reardon pressed his fingernails into his palm. Quickly he looked away from the deer, focusing his attention on the crowd in the distance. He tried to find a face to hold on to but the distance was too great, the features too blurred.

"Reardon?" Mathesson took Reardon by the arm. "Hey, you okay?"

Reardon turned away, gesturing for Mathesson to cover the body again. Mathesson swiftly obeyed and Reardon could hear the brittle sound of the tarpaulin unfolding out again, stretching over the body of the deer.

"You came back on duty too soon, John," Mathesson said. "You should have taken a little more time off. When a man loses his wife he needs some time to take it easy, to adjust. you know?"

Reardon nodded. "I'll be all right."

"Sure you will. But still, maybe you should take some extra time off."

"No," Reardon said. "It's okay."

"But . . ."

Reardon looked at him intently. "It's just a little gruesome after you've been away from it for a while." He could feel himself trembling underneath his topcoat. He thrust his hands into his coat, his fingers searching for something to distract him. He grasped a ballpoint pen in one hand and began clicking the point in and out.

"Sure it is," Mathesson said sympathetically. He smiled. "Christ, this one is a little gruesome even if you haven't been away from it."

"Uncover the other one," Reardon said.

"Go have a cup of coffee first. There's no big hurry about this, is there?"

"I want to finish it up now."

Mathesson shrugged. "Okay, John."

Slowly Mathesson made his way to the other covered body and bent down to pull the tarpaulin back. He looked at Reardon. "This one's not so bad. Not like the other one. This one went out fast."

When Mathesson pulled back the covering, Reardon saw what he meant. The deer's spine had been severed at the neck in one powerful sweep, and the blood had surged from its throat in a broad, deep wave. As Reardon had suspected, death had come instantaneously to this fallow deer.

Reardon nodded for Mathesson to cover the body and gently released the pen in his pocket.

"Now why don't you go have a cup of coffee?" Mathesson said. "All the legwork is being done. You can take a break. Nothing's going to happen in the next few minutes."

Reardon smiled. "Okay, maybe I will."

As he left the cage, Reardon's legs felt unstable under him. He was afraid and he knew that he was afraid of something that did not seem to have anything to do with the fallow deer. He was afraid of a surging feeling that had plagued him during the first years of his career, when he had walked the streets as a young policeman. In the neighborhood where he had grown up, in the destitute tenements and littered streets, there had been three avenues of escape: crime, the priesthood or the police force. He had never considered the first, but the decision to choose the police had had much of the priesthood in it. He had wanted to minister to distress, to protect helplessness and innocence from the abuse that constantly threatened them. It had been a romantic notion, and he had quickly discarded its more sentimental aspects. But something of it had always lingered in him; nothing could destroy it altogether, and Reardon sensed that he should not let it be destroyed. He suspected that this sensation of protection and guardianship formed the better part of him, and he did not want to lose it. But now its power seemed to be rising in unpredictable and uncontrollable bursts. And he was afraid.

2

In the coffee shop across from the park Reardon remembered something from his childhood. It seemed to
rise like the steam from his cup of coffee. He and his
father had been walking back from Sunday morning
Mass, his father in the one suit he owned, seemingly for
no other reason than to wear it to Mass, when his
father had stopped to buy a paper from the blind newsdealer at the corner. They had stopped a few feet beyond the stand and his father had begun to flip through
the paper when two men stepped up to the newsstand.
The man closest to the stand asked for a *Times* and put
a one-dollar bill in the blind man's hand.

"A single, sir?" the blind man asked.

"No," the man said, "a ten."

The owner smiled. "Excuse me, sir," he said and
called out into the street. "Could someone passing step
over here a minute, please?"

When the second man stepped forward and asked
what the problem was the blind man said, "Sorry to
trouble you, but could you tell me the denomination of
this bill?"

The two men looked at each other and one of them,
Reardon remembered, grinned.

"It's a ten," the second man said.

"Thank you," the blind man said and started count-
ing out change for a ten.

Reardon thought that he alone had seen the exchange. But suddenly his father dropped his newspaper and wheeled around. "Just a minute there," he said, and as the first man, startled, turned to run, Reardon saw his father pitch abruptly forward and seize the man by his coat collar.

The second man bolted and was quickly gone from sight, but Reardon's father slammed the first one up against the side wall of the newsstand and, holding him half suspended by his coat collar, stared coldly into his face. "You're a filthy pig," he said, and Reardon had been shocked by the contempt in his voice. "Only the lowest of the low would stoop to robbing a blind man." He slammed the man's head back against the wall. "Where do you live?"

Head forced back by the fists gripping the coat together under his chin, eyes bulging, the man struggled to free himself but said nothing.

Reardon's father slammed him against the newsstand wall again. "Where do you live?"

When the man didn't answer, Reardon's father suddenly released him and backhanded him across the face. Caught unprepared, the man staggered and went down on one knee, and Reardon's father seized him by the hair and, placing a knee in the small of his back, yanked his head back.

"Tell me where you live," he said contemptuously.

"110th Street," the man whimpered. "212 110th Street."

Reardon's father released his grip on the man's hair and sent him sprawling with a shove of his knee. "Get up," he said and without waiting for compliance reached down and yanked the man erect by his coat collar. "Now I know where you live," he said, "and I'll tell you something. If I ever see you around this neighborhood again, I'm going to put your little prick in a door and slam it shut." He flung the man away from him. "Now get out of here."

When it was over, Reardon remembered, after the man had fled and the newsdealer had expressed his thanks, he and his father had crossed the street into a park, his father withdrawn and silent, as if troubled by his own outburst of temper. Inside the park they sat down on a bench and his father took his hand and held it.

"I said some pretty bad things back there, Johnny," he said. "You'll have to forgive me. I was very mad." He paused a moment, examining Reardon's face. "You know I'm a policeman, don't you, son?"

"Yes, Papa."

"A policeman," his father said, "guards the world against scum like you just seen try to rob a poor blind man."

Reardon remembered how he had nodded solemnly, a child acknowledging the importance of something felt but not understood.

"Do you remember the story of Cain and Abel in the Bible?" his father asked.

"Yes, Papa."

"Well, it says how Cain killed his brother, and that was the first murder. But they don't mention them poor guys that had to track Cain down and question him until he broke down and told the truth about what he did." Reardon remembered how his father had looked intently into his eyes. "Leave the punishing to God," he had said, "but they still have to be run down. They still have to be caught."

"Yes, Papa."

Yes, Papa. Yes, Papa. Reardon nodded into the rising steam, but even now he was not sure what he had agreed to.

Mathesson seemed surprised when Reardon returned to the cage of the fallow deer. The cage was crowded now with police photographers and lab crews of various kinds, and Mathesson had to push through them to finally reach Reardon at the entrance of the cage. "I didn't think you were coming back," he said.

"I wanted to look around a little more," Reardon said.

"Look around a little more? For what? We've got teams searching everywhere."

"I just wanted to take another look."

"Okay," Mathesson said lightly. "I don't think you'll find much."

"Probably not," Reardon said. He stepped past Mathesson and into the cage of the fallow deer.

He walked to the middle of the cage and stopped. For a moment he stared straight ahead into the shed which had protected the deer from the weather, then slowly he turned to the right, his eyes scanning each side of the cage in turn, stopping occasionally to look out beyond the bars and toward the distant parts of the Children's Zoo.

His custom of revisiting the crime scene several times during the course of an investigation was not generally a search for physical evidence but for an atmosphere, a sense of how and under what conditions the violence had taken place. At times he would do no more than stare at the chalk outline of the body's position, or at a certain pattern of blood on the wall or the peculiarly savage rip of a curtain. Murder, he knew, lingered in a room like an odor, defiling and debasing everything, insisting that here within these walls something precious was unforgivably wasted. That sense of waste was murder's common legacy, and these moments were, for Reardon, part of a quest not so much for a particular murderer but for murder itself, for the murdering mind or the conditions that created it.

Finally he had made his full circle around the cage. His eyes once again rested on the shed.

"Well, find anything?" Mathesson asked, glancing up from his notebook.

"No," Reardon replied quietly. "What time were they killed?"

"Between three and three-thirty this morning," Mathesson said. "Two patrolmen named Burns and Fitzgerald answered the call, and they said that according to one of the workmen . . ." He quickly turned through his notebook. "Here it is. According to one of the workmen—a guy named Gilbert Noble—they had to have been killed between three and three-thirty this morning. He works on the night crew. He saw the deer alive at three, and he saw them dead at three-thirty. But he didn't see nothing in between."

"Nothing?"

"Nothing important. He said there were a few people in the park earlier in the evening, but that's all."

"I want to talk to him anyway."

"Okay," Mathesson said. "I'll have him come in and you can talk to him."

Reardon nodded toward the open shed. "Anybody check that place out?"

"Yeah. It's empty except for some dried leaves and deer shit. We rustled around in the leaves looking for the weapon, but there's nothing there. No bits of clothing or anything like that. It looks like the killing was done out here. Out in the open. The whole thing.

There's not a drop of blood in that whole goddamn shed."

"I'll take a quick look," Reardon said. He turned and walked toward the shed.

It was constructed of cinder blocks and was roofed with a sheet of tin. The front was entirely open and faced out toward the bars. The entire structure was covered with graffiti.

"How did all that writing get in there?" Reardon asked, stopping at the entrance of the shed.

"I think it must have happened last summer," Mathesson said. "I think Burns said the deer were taken someplace else and the bars were down for a while. They were doing some sort of maintenance work or something like that. Anyway, the bars were taken down, so the local artist community did its thing." Mathesson grinned. "Let me know if you see any hot numbers. That's how I used to get most of my dates."

A breeze suddenly skirted through the park, driving small, noisy waves of dried leaves across the cement floor of the cage. Reardon turned up the collar of his overcoat and stepped inside the shed.

Almost every square inch of the shed was covered with some kind of writing. Most prominent were the obscenities, references to various sexual acts or bodily functions. Interspersed with these were individual names, hundreds of them: Stanislas and Pedro, Betsie and Wilhelmina. There were also attempts at poetry, bits of personal philosophy and expressions of occult religions. But what grasped Reardon's attention was something else, something that stood out from the rest; most of the writing had been done with chalk or spray paint, but this one was written in a color Reardon had seen too often not to recognize.

"Mathesson!" he called. "Come in here a minute."

Mathesson came in and glanced about the shed. "What is it?"

Reardon pointed to a rusty red scrawl on the ceiling of the shed. "Doesn't that look like it's written in dried blood?"

Mathesson squinted up at the ceiling. "Yeah, it does. It looks like it could be."

"I think it is," Reardon said. "It's a roman numeral two."

"Yeah."

"I want you to have that piece of tin cut out and sent down to the lab for an analysis. I think it's blood of some kind. It may have come from the deer."

"A roman numeral two," Mathesson said thoughtfully. "Jesus Christ. What the hell could that mean?"

"I don't know. Maybe nothing. Maybe it's just a tally."

"A tally? What do you mean?"

"Just that it may be a tally and nothing else." Reardon looked up at the roman numeral two. "You know, the number 'two' for two dead deer."

"Oh," Mathesson said. "Yeah, maybe." He looked at the number, then outside at the two tarpaulins lying heavily over the bodies of the fallow deer. He shook his head. "A tally."

A tally, Reardon thought. Perhaps. But he was also thinking of another possibility. He had seen it more times than he liked to recall, and it had always begun with a terrible crime, one almost incomprehensible in its brutality: sex organs hanging from a doorknob or a severed finger floating placidly in a decanter of scotch or some other inhuman mutilation. And then that sudden, quiet, stunning touch of the human. The undeniable suggestion that even in the raging, animal cruelty of the crime, some touch of conscience remained.

Sometimes it might be nothing more than a handkerchief too obviously left behind. Once, Reardon recalled,
it was a telephone number tucked loosely under a door-
mat. But each time it had led to the killer, who had
retained, even through the viciousness of the act, the
certain knowledge that it was wrong and who was,
therefore, determined to be caught.

Or perhaps it *was* a tally, and nothing more.

When Reardon got back to his desk in the precinct
house, he found a note requesting him to telephone his
son. He felt no desire to call but found himself dialing
his son's law office, anyway.

"Mr. Reardon's office," the secretary said.

"This is his father," Reardon said.

"He's in conference at this time."

"This is his father," Reardon repeated. He had sat
through too many conferences in his life to be awed by
the word.

There was a pause. "Uh, just a moment, sir. I'll see
if he can be interrupted."

Reardon waited for a moment, thinking of the fallow
deer with more than a trace of pity, then of a small
dog he had once owned. It had been run over by a car.
The driver had stopped, gotten out and very sadly offered his apologies and some money. Reardon had de-
clined, and they had shaken hands. Whenever Reardon
felt some need for a quiet moment of shared decency
and generosity, his mind turned to that.

"Mr. Reardon?" the secretary said, returning to the
line.

"Yes."

"Mr. Reardon wishes to know if you will have dinner with him tonight. He would like you to come to his
apartment at around seven-thirty."

"All right," Reardon said.

"May I tell him you'll be there?"

Reardon found the formality of the secretary irritating. "Yes, you may."

"Thank you, sir."

"Yeah, right," Reardon hastily said, glad to get off the phone.

As soon as he hung up he went into Piccolini's office. Piccolini sat hunched over his desk, staring glumly at an inch-thick stack of requisition forms. Through the window at Piccolini's back Reardon could see a few flakes of falling snow. "I saw the deer," Reardon said.

"Get any leads?" Piccolini was smoking an enormous black cigar, and the entire room was filled with heavy blue smoke.

"Maybe one."

Piccolini's eyes brightened. "Yeah, what?"

"There was some writing on the shed."

"What kind of writing?"

"A roman numeral two."

Piccolini squinted through a puff of smoke. "What does that mean?"

"I don't know," Reardon said. "I'm having the lab check to see if it was written in deer's blood."

"Is that all?"

"One of the deer died instantly," Reardon added dryly.

Piccolini leaned forward in his chair. "Reardon, I told you this is an important case. This may be the biggest thing in the city right now. Are you taking this thing seriously?"

"Yes."

"You retire in four years, Reardon."

"So?"

"So you have a great record with the department.

The Lamprey case alone would get you into the detectives' hall of fame."

Reardon shrugged. "The Lamprey case was luck."

"The Lamprey case was memory," Piccolini said, "remembering details from way back. That's what a detective is all about."

Reardon did not know where this was supposed to be leading. Rehashing old cases had never appealed to him. It was like listening to middle-aged former quarterbacks blathering about past athletic glories. He looked out beyond Piccolini's face and through the window behind him to the snow.

"You know you retire in a few years," Piccolini said, "so go out on a big one. Don't mess this up. It's a big case. It's not a homicide, but it's a big case, like I keep telling you. So break it. Go out a champ."

"Save the locker room pep talk, Mario. I'm too old to get steam out of that stuff."

"Maybe so, but I'd hate for you to louse this up."

"It won't be loused up."

"Good."

Reardon went back to his desk and began typing up a brief account of his investigation so far. He described the condition of the deer, recorded the probable time of death, noted the probable characteristics of the death weapon or weapons. He noted that entry into the cage of the fallow deer would have been possible for anyone within the normal range of height and weight, that no human bloodstains had been located at or near the scene of the crime, and that, thus far, there were no witnesses.

He had recorded such details hundred of times. He had described warehouses of weaponry: pistols of all calibers, shotguns of all gauges, blades of all lengths and widths and adornment, spikes, tire irons, bottles of all shapes and colors, acids, poisons, ropes, chains, wires, torches, bricks, baseball bats—every conceivable object that an agile, enraged and premeditating ape could use to kill another.

He sat, thinking over the details of the case before him, but they did not seem to lead anywhere. Wallace Van Allen had donated two fallow deer and someone had killed them both, one with a ferocious brutality and the other with one devastating blow. Perhaps the killer had been repelled by his slaughter of the first deer and then had impulsively killed the other one out of some deranged fear of leaving any witness, even an animal. Or perhaps the approach of a human witness had frightened him, causing him to cut short the slaughter he had intended for the second deer. If he had bolted from the park someone might have noticed him. And Reardon knew he must have been drenched with blood after the first killing. A slashing killing sent geysers of blood in all directions; spurting vessels, the arcs of the weapon in its rise and fall, the thrashing about of the victim—every act in a slashing killing left a trail of blood. But no amount of blood caked on a killer or oozing from between his fingers would matter if there were no one around to see it. And as yet there were no witnesses. Reardon had already recorded that intolerable fact succinctly in his notebook: "Wit.: 0."

The crime had taken place at about three-thirty in the morning. Still, Reardon's experience had taught him that eyes watched the streets constantly, that in a large city in a public place there were almost no unrecorded acts. He remembered the Ruiz case. If anyone had ever expected to kill invisibly in a city it was Paco Ruiz. Dressed in a business suit although he was a blue-collar worker, Ruiz had escorted a teenage boy to the depths of the city's largest park and in one of its many narrow ravines of granite and underbrush he had soundlessly strangled him to death. It had happened about two hours before dawn on a moonless night in the heart of a supposedly deserted and isolated park, and two separate people had seen it. One was another teenage boy who had run away from his home that afternoon, fleeing the alcoholic rage of his father. The other was a thirty-five-year-old painter who all his life, he told Reardon, had been looking for the darkest place in the world in order to get some understanding of the nature of light. Each witness had been unaware of the other, but both of them had watched Ruiz and the boy approach from the distance, and both had sat in horrified astonishment and watched, from two widely separate angles, a large muscular man strangle a small-framed boy to death.

In any event, Reardon thought, it was too early to tell if there were any witnesses to what had happened in the cage of the fallow deer between three and three-thirty in the morning. Sometimes it took a very long time for witnesses to come forward. Sometimes they never did. Reardon did not intend to become impatient.

3

Reardon arrived at his son's apartment at exactly seven-thirty. He did not want to spend any more time there than he had to. He had admitted to himself some years ago that he did not like his son very much anymore, or his son's wife or children or friends. They lived in one of the more fashionable areas of the city, where every door had a doorman, and Reardon always felt an intense discomfort at having a man his own age, gray and rather used-up and dressed clownishly in an absurdly ornate uniform, open the door for him, smile artificially and blurt, "Good evening, sir." But this was evidently what his son wanted; it had propelled him to win his Ivy League scholarship, perform masterfully in college, and then seek out and secure a position in what Reardon was told was one of the city's most prestigious law firms. But in the process of all that, Reardon thought, Timothy had lost the ability to distinguish between the things that really mattered in life and those that only seemed to.

Abbey answered the door. "Well, hello, papa," she said.

She was young; that was the most significant thing about her. She had borne two children but still managed to retain a kind of teenage ebullience. Everything she said, she said with enthusiasm; every gesture had a synaptic energy of its own. Her lithe body made Rear-

41

don feel dense and heavy. Just being around her made him feel tired.

Reardon removed his hat. "Hi," he said. He did not feel like the bouncy, lovable, garrulous old grandpa he knew she expected him to be.

Abbey took Reardon by the arm and escorted him into the living room of the apartment. It was a place of pastels. Pastel blue walls. Pastel upholstery on the chairs and sofa. Even the paintings were pastel, little girls in soft-colored dresses, their cheeks lightly flushed with pink.

"You look tired," she said after they had both sat down. "Have you been eating regularly?"

Reardon tried to make a joke to please and relieve her. "I eat regularly, six times a day," he said, smiling ludicrously as he patted himself on the stomach.

"Weight becomes you," Abbey said.

Suddenly Reardon remembered her at Millie's funeral, remembered the pained expression that had passed over her face when Timothy had performed his counterfeit of grief. Impulsively, he leaned over and kissed her cheek.

"Well, thank you," she said lightly, but Reardon could tell that something in his gesture had alarmed her.

"I have moments . . ." Reardon heard himself say, knowing that his sudden gesture of affection had surged up from that other part of him that frightened him with its power. "I have moments . . ." he began again, but the rest of the sentence died in his mouth.

"What?" she asked, clearly concerned now.

"Nothing."

"Are you all right?"

Reardon tried to smile. "Yes, I'm all right." He felt sorry that he had lost control, had imposed himself upon her lightheartedness and goodwill.

"Really?" Abbey said. "You sure?"

Reardon forced a laugh. "Of course, of course. Can't an old man kiss a lovely young lady?"

"Sure," Abbey said brightly. She leaned forward and kissed him. "Can a young lady kiss a great-looking father-in-law?"

"Sure," Reardon said.

"Timothy will be in in a moment," she said. "Would you like a drink?"

"Irish whiskey."

"I'll get it."

She left the room, and Reardon could hear her talking to his son in the next room. There seemed to be some urgency in their voices, but he could not tell what it was all about. He looked down at his hat. Gray and weathered, it looked incongruous on the expensive chair with its lavender silk upholstery. He felt like an intruder, a poor relation swept up to their apartment by some sudden calamity—fire or flood or worse. He did not belong there with the luxurious furniture, the marble and the lace and the delicate vases with flower designs. In his life he had been invited to such rooms only when a dead body lay on the floor, its blood silently staining the Oriental rug.

"How are you, Father?" Timothy asked as he entered the room. He wore a dark-gray pinstripe suit. Below the coat a vest was drawn primly over his stomach. His tie was pulled tightly against his throat as if he were going to a corporate board meeting. He had recently taken to calling Reardon "father," rather than the more familiar "papa."

"Hello, Tim," Reardon said.

"How are you?" Timothy sat down in a chair opposite Reardon and sipped casually from a martini glass.

"Fine. Where are the children?"

"At the symphony."

Reardon nodded, wondering who had taken them, since both parents were at home. But then, he recalled, times were different now; people could be hired to do such things.

"Well, do you like being back at work?" Timothy asked.

Reardon nodded.

Timothy took a long, dark cigar from his coat pocket and handed it to Reardon.

"No, thanks," Reardon said.

"What? My father turning down a good cigar?"

"I've quit smoking."

"Really? Well, give it to one of your associates."

Associates? thought Reardon. "No," he said, "keep it."

"Very well," Timothy said. "I don't smoke them, as you know, but I thought you might like it. Very expensive, you know."

"It would probably be too strong for me, anyway," Reardon said dryly.

Timothy slapped his knees lightly and smiled. "Well, now, how are things on the force?"

"Same as always."

"Murder and mayhem, I suppose."

"The usual."

"Ever thought of an early retirement?"

Here it comes again, Reardon thought. "I like to work, Tim," he said. "I don't want to retire. I've told you that before. What would I do? What is it you think I would do if I retired?"

"Anything," Timothy said. He raised his arm and gently massaged the back of his neck while he stared absently into Reardon's face.

"No," Reardon said. "I'm not looking forward to retirement. I'll leave when they make me leave."

"Still the same old hardtack," Timothy said.

"Maybe. Is my whiskey almost ready?"

"Sure, Abbey will bring it in shortly. We don't drink Irish whiskey around here, so you should take the bottle with you when you go. It just sits here. Nobody drinks it."

"I have a bottle at home," Reardon said. He did not want his son's Irish whiskey, or his son's financial support for retirement, or his son's way of life.

Timothy nodded and leaned back in his chair. He seemed as exhausted and impatient with their conversation as Reardon was.

"How's your work coming?" Reardon asked dutifully.

"Fine, fine," Timothy said. "But sometimes I think our firm should employ some detectives to help us with some of our cases. You know, old-fashioned street cops like yourself who can slice through all the rhetoric and get to the meat of the thing."

"The what?"

"The rhetoric," Timothy said, "slice through the rhetoric."

Reardon nodded.

"Some of the lawyers on my staff are ineffective at investigation and research. Everything has to be laid out for them."

Reardon nodded.

"They aren't self-motivated. They have to be told everything. No initiative."

Reardon nodded. "Maybe so," he said.

That night Reardon had the first dream he could remember in many years. He was sitting on a beach in the fog, smoking a cigarette, when a woman's body floated quietly up on shore. She lay facedown at his feet, the top of her head resting easily on the tip of his shoe. Her hair was long and red and she was wearing a flowered dress. A tide gently swept a single strand of pearls from under her neck and then drew it back again.

In the dream Reardon was not at all shocked or frightened by the body. It had seemed to come on shore as naturally as a wave, and he stared at it without emotion, as if it were no more than a brightly colored shell. His eyes moved calmly over her dress. He noted the flowers in the design, small red rose buds alternating in diagonal lines with rows of pink dogwood petals. He remembered that he had seen this same dress in a shop window at the corner of 60th Street and Second Avenue almost twenty-five years before and had almost bought it for his wife's birthday. He wondered how many such dresses had been made and in how many shops they had been sold. He bent over and started to look for a label, but in so doing he touched the woman's bright-red hair, and a blade of terror pierced his loins and drove upward into his brain. Instantly he tried to run, but the hair transformed itself into a claw and seized his hand and began dragging him into the water. Frantically he tried to pull free, but the claw gripped his hand like a steel vise, and by the time his first scream broke through the fog he was waist-deep in the sea. His eyes ravaged the shore for someone to rescue him, looking for help, overturning garbage cans and stripping wharves. They burned off the surrounding fog and split open the dunes and over-turned the cottages behind them, but still there was no one to save him. His last scream was stifled by the salt water flooding his mouth as he went down.

Reardon woke, gasping for breath, his hand groping in the darkness, at last finding the light switch near his bed. For a while he sat up in bed and allowed his eyes to roam about the room, rooting his mind once again in the familiar, comfortable objects around him. But he could not find comfort in them. He felt almost like an intruder in his own room, as if the old brown suit that hung in his closet had been molded to the body of some other man more composed than himself. He rested his head in his cupped hands and waited for dawn.

4

The next morning Reardon did not go directly to the precinct headquarters. Instead, he walked to the Children's Zoo. For a while he sat on a bench opposite the cage of the fallow deer. The bodies had been taken away, and the cages had been meticulously washed of all signs of the violence that had taken place before dawn on Monday morning.

He gazed around the park, trying to determine in which direction the killer might have fled. Then he looked beyond the bars to the chalk-drawn positions where the bodies had been found. The back of the cage was a solid stone wall almost fifteen feet high. Without a ladder or a rope no one could have climbed over it. But in front of the cage two sidewalks led in different directions. The one to the right turned into a winding trail that eventually led all the way to the opposite side of the park. The other led directly to a flight of stairs which ascended to Fifth Avenue. The killer would have taken the route through the park, Reardon thought. He shrugged. It was a mundane assumption. Bloodied as he must have been, of course the killer would not have lurched up onto Fifth Avenue, even between three and three-thirty in the morning.

"Morning, John," Mathesson said. He stood towering over Reardon, a breeze gently flapping the collar of his coat. He brought his large hands out of his coat pockets and pressed his hat more firmly down on his head.

Reardon had not seen him approach. "Hello, Jack," he said.

"Trying to think like a freako this morning?"

"No," Reardon said. "I'm trying to think like an inexperienced murderer."

"So what did you come up with?"

Reardon smiled at the absurdity of what he had come up with. "That the killer probably took the trail through the park rather than the stairs to Fifth Avenue."

Mathesson laughed. "That ought to get you a citation," he said. "How are you this morning, John?"

Reardon knew Mathesson was still bothered by his response to the deer on Monday morning. "I'm fine."

"Get a good night's sleep?"

"I guess," Reardon said. He looked at the cage again. "Did you check with the precinct this morning?"

"Yeah."

"Anything interesting?"

"Well, the lab is finished with the autopsy on the deer. There were fifty-seven wounds on one of them and just that one on the other."

"Anything else?"

"Yeah, they're bringing out another crew to look for the weapon. I guess the first crew just did a quick search. Anyway, the first group didn't come up with anything, so they're sending out another one."

"Since when do they send out two separate crews to search for a weapon?" Reardon asked.

Mathesson smiled. "Since Wallace Van Allen got his deer sliced up, that's since when." He glanced resentfully at the great houses and luxury hotels that towered over the park. "Don't this goddamn hubbub about a couple of animals seem a little much to you?"

"I suppose."

"Two deer!" Mathesson said. "Can you believe that? Can you believe the amount of trouble and expense the department's going to when it's not even a murder case yet?"

Reardon said nothing.

"Two lousy deer. And you'd think it was the only crime in the city." He shrugged and changed the subject. "What's your plan for today?"

"I don't know for sure," Reardon said.

"That ought to please Piccolini."

"What would you suggest then?"

Mathesson placed his hands in his overcoat pockets and looked helplessly at Reardon.

"Crews are covering the area looking for witnesses, right?" Reardon asked.

"Right."

"And they haven't come up with any, right?"

"Right."

"And crews are looking for the weapon, right? And they haven't found it yet, right?"

"Yeah," Mathesson said.

"And there must be crews keeping it out of the papers for a while, right?"

Mathesson smiled and said, "Right."

"Okay, that's it. No witnesses, no weapon and no publicity."

"How about the wounds?" Mathesson asked. "Could they mean anything?"

"What?"

"I don't know."

"Fifty-seven wounds on one body and just one on the other?" Reardon said. "You're grabbing for straws, and that's always a mistake."

"Yeah," Mathesson said. He sat down next to Reardon. "Two lousy deer." He leaned back, arms stretched casually along the backrest of the bench, and stared up through the trees. "You know, old Wallace himself could have been a pretty good witness if he had some binoculars."

"What do you mean?"

Mathesson pointed to a line of trees at the top of a twenty-five-story apartment house overlooking Fifth Avenue. "See those trees, the ones on top of that building?"

"Yeah," Reardon answered.

"That's the Van Allen penthouse."

Reardon stared for a moment at the building. He could tell that the wind was rustling through the trees that grew incongruously and imperiously hundreds of feet above Fifth Avenue.

When Reardon returned to the precinct house later that morning, he reviewed the arrest sheet for the previous day. For the last twenty-four hours people had been molesting each other in the accustomed fashion. They had been stealing from and killing each other, raping and falsely accusing each other, and running out on debts. Someone named Bill Robbins had attacked his mother with a ballpoint pen in a restaurant on 79th Street. Two teenagers named Thompson and Berger had drunkenly run down a pedestrian on Second Avenue. A homosexual had propositioned a plainclothes officer in the washroom of Grand Central Station. Two construction workers had wrecked a bar on First Avenue. At another bar a few blocks away an off-duty policeman had beaten his wife to a pulp in full view of twenty-seven people. Some of them had still been cheering him on when patrolmen arrived and arrested everyone, spectators included, for disorderly conduct.

Reardon wearily ran his fingers through his hair and continued reading the arrest sheet, his eyes reviewing the crimes, roaming up and down the streets and avenues where they were committed, through the roster of whores, pimps, muggers, purse snatchers and drunks, through the embittered marriages, the turncoat friends, amateur arsonists, and everywhere through hopelessly flailing rage. But he did not stop. He was looking for something, and about two-thirds down the third page he found it. The first thing he noticed was the place the arrest had been made: the steps leading up to the Fifth Avenue entrance of the Central Park Zoo on 64th Street. Quickly, he ran his finger across the page for the time of the arrest: Monday . . . 3:35 A.M. There was little other information available on the report. Someone named Winthrop Lewis Daniels had been arrested for possession of cocaine.

Reardon looked up from his desk. "Mathesson," he called. He saw Mathesson turn away from the water cooler in the hall and approach his desk.

"I got something here," Reardon said.

Mathesson was smiling. "Find some more blood?"

Reardon handed him the arrest sheet. "About a third of the way up from the bottom. That cocaine bust. Take a look at that."

"Winthrop Lewis Daniels," Mathesson said. He looked at Reardon. "Who's that?"

"I don't know, but look at where that bust was made. Look at when it was made."

Mathesson's eyes returned to the sheet, widened in recognition. "Well, I'll be goddamned. That puts that hophead close to the deer, don't it. Shit, he couldn't have been more than two or three blocks away."

"That's right."

Mathesson smiled. "Now wouldn't that be a lucky break."

"It says Langhof made that bust," Reardon said. "Is he around the precinct house?"

"He's upstairs."

"Tell him I want to talk to him."

When Mathesson had gone Reardon looked at the arrest sheet again. He took a map of Central Park from one of his desk drawers and unfolded it on his desk. The map confirmed what he already knew: that Daniels had been arrested two blocks away from the cages of the fallow deer maybe five minutes or so after they had been killed.

He heard steps coming down the stairway at the rear of the precinct house and turned to see Mathesson and Langhof approaching his desk. Langhof was dressed in a neatly pressed uniform, his cap blocked squarely on his head, with the badge shining brightly from his chest like a small golden flame.

"Mathesson here says you want to talk to me," he said.

"Yeah," Reardon said. "I want to talk to you about that cocaine bust you made yesterday."

"What about it?"

"Where did you pick Daniels up?"

Langhof looked at Reardon suspiciously. "Right on Fifth Avenue. Why?"

Reardon reversed the map on his desk so that Langhof could read it. "Where on Fifth Avenue?"

Langhof placed his finger directly on the steps at 64th Street. "Right there."

"On the steps?"

"Yeah. Right on the steps."

"The arrest sheet said you busted him at 3:35 A.M. on Monday morning. Is that right?"

Langhof looked at Reardon. "That's *exactly* right. I'm always real careful about the time. I *always* get that right. A lot depends on that."

"What was Daniels doing?" Mathesson asked.

"He was standing on top of the stairs. He was kind of leaning on that stone pillar at the top."

"Just leaning?"

"No, he wasn't just leaning!" snapped Langhof. "He was snorting coke, the stupid little fuck."

"On the street?"

"Right there on Fifth Avenue," Langhof said. "We cruised right up to him in the patrol car. I just kind of looked out the window, just glancing out, you know, not really looking for anything, and there he was. Snorting right on the fucking street." He shook his head in amazement. "I couldn't believe it. I thought maybe this was some kind of joke, a come-on, you know, some kind of April fool type thing to make us look stupid. I tapped my partner and pointed to this guy. I says, 'Do you think that's for real?' I couldn't believe that a guy would just stand around on the street and snort coke. Not even at three or four in the morning."

Mathesson smiled. "So what did he say, your partner?"

"He said we'd better find out."

Mathesson seemed delighted with the story. "Then what happened?"

"We both got out of the car. We just strolled over to this guy—what's his name?—Daniels. We just strolled over to him."

"He didn't try to get away?"

"Get away?" Langhof laughed. "He didn't even know we were around till we were right under his goddamn nose. He was too busy with that fucking coke. He was really into it, you know." Langhof grinned. "Dumb bastard. No. Not dumb. He just didn't give a shit. We asked him what he was doing, and he just looked at us. You know, like we were garbage, like what the hell was it our business what he was doing." He looked at Reardon. "I never seen such a thing in my life. I mean there this little prick was, snorting coke like a bastard, and he just looks at us like we come from Mars or something, like we was spoiling his good time, you know?"

Reardon nodded.

"Then what happened?" Mathesson asked.

"Then my partner says, 'What you got there, buddy?' and he still didn't say nothing. He just stared at us. So I grabbed the bag. The coke was in a little cellophane pouch. So I grabbed it. I took a sniff. Coke. So we busted his little ass."

"You took him to the precinct house?" Reardon asked.

"Yeah, we shoved him in the patrol car, told him his rights and all that shit, and took him right to the precinct house. And we didn't touch that little prick either," Langhof blurted suddenly, angrily. "So if this little third degree we're having is about police brutality, you can forget it."

"What makes you think this has anything to do with something like that?" Reardon asked.

"Well, that's the way it goes, ain't it?" Langhof said.

"What do you mean?"

"Look, the minute we got that little fucker to the precinct house he says he wants to call his old man. So we let him. That's his right, right? So we let him. And Jesus Christ, there was three goddamn lawyers down here before we could get the arrest report written out. He was on the streets again in no time."

"You boys better watch out who you fuck with on

the east side of Central Park," Mathesson kidded. "You'll be the ones that end up getting your asses busted."

"Well, it was a solid bust," Langhof said bitterly, "a solid goddamn bust, whether it sticks or not. No matter what you guys report."

"We're not trying to break your bust," Reardon said.

"You're not?"

"No, we're not."

Langhof seemed to relax. "Hell, I figured the department was embarrassed by it, or something, afraid of all those lawyers or something like that."

"No," Mathesson said, "we're checking into something else. We don't give a shit about this bust."

"Did you notice anything strange about Daniels?" Reardon asked.

"No." Langhof scratched his head, subdued now. "No, nothing that I can think of except the way he just didn't seem to care about us, about being busted."

"Did you notice if he looked out of breath, tired, anything like that?" Reardon asked.

"No."

"How about blood?" Mathesson asked. "Did you notice any blood on him?"

"Blood?"

"Yeah, blood."

"No, we didn't see no blood. This guy was very straight-looking. Well dressed. He could have walked right out of a TV commercial. He was no slob." Langhof stared at Reardon curiously. "What is it with this guy anyway?"

"Reardon thought he might have had something to do with the deer killing," Mathesson said.

"The deer were killed between three and three-thirty the same morning you made the bust," Reardon said.

"Daniels could have been involved in it and still be on Fifth Avenue by the time you busted him. Or he could have seen something. Maybe he came through the park, you know? He might have passed the deer cages just about the time they were being killed."

Langhof shook his head. "Well, he didn't look like he could have killed no deer. He didn't have no blood on him or look tired or anything like that. He was too cool, man. That's what we noticed the most. And he didn't have no blood on him."

"You sure?" Mathesson said.

"Hell, yes. Come on, Mathesson, don't you think we'd have noticed something like that?"

"Where is this Daniels now?" Reardon asked.

"At home, I guess." Langhof pulled a notebook from his back pocket and flipped through it. "Here it is. He lives at Thirty-one East Sixty-Eighth Street."

"Any apartment number?"

"No, it's a townhouse I guess."

Reardon wrote the address in his notebook. "Okay. Thanks."

"What do you think?" Mathesson asked Reardon after Langhof had gone back upstairs.

"About what?"

"About this guy Daniels?"

"I don't know for sure," Reardon said quietly, "but I want to talk to him."

Mathesson grinned. "You'd better take a dozen or so lawyers with you before you try that."

Reardon did not smile. "Maybe so."

"I'll go talk to Langhof's partner," Mathesson said. "Maybe he noticed something."

"Okay," Reardon said. "Have him go through the whole thing, just like Langhof."

"Right."

After Mathesson had gone, Reardon sat down at his desk and looked at the map again, running his fingers back and forth over the inch of space that divided the stairs at Fifth Avenue from the cages of the fallow deer. He remembered Langhof's description of Daniels as the two patrolmen had approached him, the way he had leaned casually at the top of the stairs, the way he seemed to regard the police as little more than a brief, irritating intrusion. He wondered how much money it took to buy confidence like that.

Reardon planned to spend the rest of the afternoon interviewing two of the three members of the night crew assigned to the Children's Zoo. The third regular member, Andros Petrakis, had been working only irregularly of late, since the illness of his wife often made it necessary for him to remain at home. On the Sunday afternoon prior to the killing Petrakis' daughter had informed the Parks Department that her father would not be coming to work his shift but that he hoped to be back at work within a few days. Consequently, only two people had been scheduled to work in the Children's Zoo the morning the fallow deer were killed.

Reardon's first interview was with Gilbert Noble, who had spoken to the patrolmen called to the scene. He was a large black man who had worked for the Parks Department for twelve years. Reardon's preliminary investigation had established that Noble had no criminal record and that he had never been treated for emotional problems of any kind. He had been hospitalized once for an injury sustained while at work as an employee of the Parks Department, but the department had paid all of Noble's hospital expenses, as well as his salary during hospitalization. There was no reason to suspect that he held any animosity toward the Parks Department.

"You were working in the Zoo the night the fallow deer were killed, is that right, Mr. Noble?" Reardon began.

Noble sat opposite Reardon, his eyes darting from one corner of the room to another. He was nervous, but that was common. In itself, it meant nothing. "That's right," he said.

"Were you in the Zoo at around three-thirty on Monday morning?" Reardon tried to make his voice as casual as he could.

"Yeah," Noble said. "Yeah, I was there. I was in the zoo. I got to work a little before midnight."

"Where were you in the zoo at about that time?"

"I was cleaning the elephant cages."

Reardon jotted Noble's answer down in his notebook. "Where are they located?" he asked in the same casual tone with which he might have asked directions from a stranger on the street.

"They're at the far end of the zoo, behind a big building. The elephants stay in that building at night."

"How long would you say you were working in the elephant cages?"

"Maybe a half hour or so. Maybe a little more."

"From when to when?"

"From about three to three-thirty."

"Did you see anybody in the zoo during that time?"

"No, I didn't see anybody. I didn't see nothing while I was in them elephant cages or on the way to them either. I would have remembered seeing anybody in the zoo around then. Ain't nobody in the zoo that time of night."

"Did you hear anything while you worked at the elephant cages?" Reardon asked.

"No."

"Anything at all?"

"No." Noble paused, gazed toward the ceiling. "Well . . ."

"Anything at all," Reardon said, "no matter how insignificant it might seem to you."

"Well, you know," Noble said slowly, "I think I did hear something while I was working with them elephants. I'd say it was about . . . let me see, well, about three o'clock or a little after. Had to be before three-thirty, though."

"What was it you heard?"

"Well, just a kind of scuffing sound, like something being pushed or dragged on the ground, on the pavement, maybe." Noble thought for a moment. "I mean, really there was kind of two different sounds."

"Two sounds?"

"Yeah. One was like . . . like metal being pushed or dragged along the sidewalk. But the other sound was kind of muffled, you know?"

"Did you hear them at the same time?"

"Yeah, right at the same time. Right together."

"So whatever was being dragged or pushed was partly covered and partly not covered."

"That might be right," Noble said. "I don't know if it means anything or not."

Reardon smiled. "Maybe not," he said, "but we like to know all the details. Do you know where the sound came from?"

"I don't know for sure," Noble said. "It was just on the other side of the elephant house, that's all. But I could hear it pretty good. It's real quiet in the zoo at that time of the morning and the sounds only lasted a few minutes. I didn't pay much attention. But it wasn't like a continuous sound. You'd hear it, then it would stop."

"There was a pause in between the sounds?"

"Yeah," Noble said, "like a pause. First you'd hear it, then it would stop, then you'd hear it again."

"How long did this sound last? How long did you hear it?"

"Just a little while."

"It passed then?"

"Yeah."

Reardon nodded and jotted in his notebook. "Did you hear anything else while you were there?"

"No, I don't think so."

"When did you find the fallow deer?"

"About three-thirty. I went to see if Bryant was around. I figured since Petrakis was out again—I mean, since he wasn't going to come to work—well, maybe Bryant would help me do the deer cage."

"Clean it?"

"Yeah, clean it."

"Was Bryant around?"

"I didn't see him."

"Where was he?"

Noble shrugged. "I don't know. Probably working somewhere else around."

"So you went to clean the deer cage yourself?"

"Yeah."

"And you found them?"

Noble grimaced. "It was terrible," he said. "They was beat up awful bad. Just awful. Blood everywhere. I never seen nothing like it."

"Yes," Reardon said. "What did you do when you found them like that?"

"I called the police."

"Immediately?"

"Yeah. I run right to the little workroom in the main building and called the cops. I was real scared myself, you know? I mean, I figured that a guy that would do that to them deer might hang around and do it to a person just as easy, you know? So I just wanted the cops to get on over there in a hurry."

"Did you see anyone at all in the zoo between, say, midnight and three in the morning?"

"Sure," Noble said, "there was a couple making out on the bench across from the bird house till about two-thirty."

"Did you see them leave?"

"Yeah. They went up the stairs to Fifth Avenue."

"What did they look like?"

"They looked like Puerto Ricans to me," Noble said with a little grin.

"Anything unusual about them?"

"No. Nothing that I can remember. Just a couple making out."

"Anybody else?"

"An old man. I remember thinking that that was odd. You know, old people don't usually come out that time of night."

"When was he there?"

"Same time as those Puerto Ricans. He came by just before they left."

"Did he stop?"

"No, he just kept walking right through the zoo and up to Fifth Avenue. He was walking kind of fast. I guess he was a little afraid of being out that time of night."

"Did anything strike you as unusual about him?" Reardon asked.

"No. And those were the only people I saw."

"And you're sure that all of them had left the zoo by two-thirty?"

"Yeah, as far as I know, they was all gone. I didn't see nobody except Bryant after that."

The interrogation lasted for another hour. Reardon went over each detail again. He went over the sounds Noble had heard. He asked him to describe the couple. He took him back through his statements about the old man he claimed to have seen and asked him if he knew whether or not either the couple or the old man had gone into any of the buildings on Fifth Avenue. Noble said that they had simply disappeared up the stairs and he had not seen them again. Had he seen any of them before in the zoo? No. Had he noticed anyone spending a lot of time at or near the cage of the fallow deer? No. Reardon asked him what he knew about his fellow workers. Harry Bryant, Noble said, was a "funny guy" who constantly made jokes about the animals, particularly when they were in the process of copulation. Did Bryant show any resentment toward his work? No. Toward the animals? No. Did he ever drink on duty? No. Andros Petrakis was "a nervous type" who did not say much. But as far as Noble knew, Petrakis liked his work, enjoyed the animals as much as could be expected and bore no grudges related to the zoo.

After Noble left, Reardon reviewed the notes he had taken during the questioning. The interrogation of Gilbert Noble had established at least one possibility. If the scuffing sounds that Noble heard were not made by the killer but by someone else, then it was possible that the unknown person might have seen the killing. But what could have made the sounds Noble described? Reardon thought they could have been made by a man with a limp dragging one foot behind him after each step. But there were two sounds, one metallic and harsh and the other muffled, and they had occurred simultaneously. In that case, Reardon thought, Noble may have actually heard the killer dragging two weapons behind him as he walked, one of them wrapped in something, the other uncovered. But the sounds Noble described were not continuous, like objects being dragged. Instead, they were interrupted by pauses.

Reardon went into Piccolini's office and told him what Noble had described. Piccolini leaned back in his chair and chewed a cigar. Anything less than an arrest seemed uninteresting to him.

"So what do you make of it?" he asked after Reardon had finished.

"I really don't know," Reardon said.

Piccolini crushed the stub of his cigar into the ashtray on his desk. "Mr. Van Allen has asked to speak with the head of the investigation. He wants a firsthand report. I made an appointment for you to see him at three-thirty this afternoon."

"Schedule him for tomorrow morning," Reardon said. "I'm seeing Bryant this afternoon."

"No," Piccolini said. "Schedule Bryant for tomorrow morning."

"Look, Mario, if Noble heard something it's just possible that Bryant *saw* something."

"It can wait."

"You've been a detective a long time," Reardon said. "You know better than that."

Piccolini opened a desk drawer, pulled out some papers and threw them on his desk. He started shuffling through them. "Bryant will have to wait," he said.

Reardon shrugged. "All right. When is Van Allen coming over?"

"He's not coming over here. You're going over there."

"Where?"

"His place on Fifth Avenue. Right across from the zoo." Piccolini took a small piece of paper and started to write down Van Allen's address.

"I know where it is," Reardon said brusquely, and turned to leave the office. For the first time in all the years he'd worked for Piccolini, he did not close the door behind him.

5

On his way over to the Van Allen penthouse later in the afternoon Reardon was waiting on the curb at the corner of 68th Street and Park Avenue when the orange "Don't Walk" sign across the wide avenue changed to "Walk." He stepped off the curb, and at that instant—and for only a brief moment—he did not know where he was. He looked around in dismay, as if he had been suddenly placed in an unfamiliar universe. The city had taken on an immense and terrifying aspect, its sounds rushing at him like famished beasts. The moment passed so quickly that he did not even have time to tremble or call out, but the terror—as it passed—was overwhelmingly real.

As he walked across Park Avenue, shaken by the experience, the feeling of having blacked out, if only momentarily, made him think of the Arturo case. He remembered Arturo as a slim, awkward young man who wore an enormous pair of black-framed glasses and seemed extremely interested in police work. For months he had haunted the station house. Week after week Arturo would go directly to the desk sergeant and be waved through the outer vestibule and up the stairs to where the precinct records were kept. He was thought to be a graduate student researching some phase of urban police work. But Benedict Arturo, all those weeks he sat poring over the precinct files, was instead investigating himself—quietly, methodically assembling the evidence that would alter his life forever, evidence from which Reardon had later learned Arturo's story.

As a child Arturo had sometimes experienced blackouts. At first these periods were short, no more than a few minutes. But by the time he entered college he was experiencing amnesiac lapses which sometimes lasted as long as seven hours. He could not recall anything that happened to him during these lapses, although friends subsequently assured him that they had seen him eating quietly in the cafeteria or strolling the halls of the library.

Although confused and frightened by these lapses, Arturo chose to ignore them. Then late one evening he awoke from one of them to find his face badly scratched. He discovered unexplained rips in his clothing, mud on his shoes. After that strange articles began appearing in his room, each time following a period of amnesia. Once it was a red handbag slung over his bedpost. On another occasion he found a single brown high-heel shoe standing upright just inside his door.

Reardon had always thought that it would not be unusual for an individual faced with things so bizarre to force them from his mind and ignore them. After all, his own wife, Millie, had ignored the cancer she knew was killing her. But Benedict Arturo did not do that. He made charts listing every quarter hour of every day. He carried them with him everywhere, marking the passage of each fifteen minutes. In this way he was able to closely approximate the times during which he was not conscious of his acts. He then compared these times with newspaper reports of crimes, particularly assaults on women. Those details that he could not get from the newspapers he obtained from precinct records. Slowly, meticulously, he convicted himself of at least six assaults, one of which had ended in a brutal murder. The document that emerged from this investigation of himself was a peculiar, brilliant masterpiece of self-incrimination. He turned it over to the police as he might have submitted a master's thesis. Then he took himself to Bellevue and committed himself to a mental institution for the criminally insane.

Until now Reardon had never believed that Arturo was quite as mad as he had seemed. He could accept irresistible compulsions; but to kill while totally unaware, that was further than Reardon had allowed himself to go. Then he had stood on a corner he had passed a thousand times and had not known where he was. It was no comfort to know that anything was possible.

Before going up to the Van Allen penthouse he walked to the zoo and sat down again on a bench across from the cage of the fallow deer. He reviewed what he had: two dead deer, a sound heard by an employee of the zoo, a couple kissing, and an old man walking quickly through the zoo before the killings; no weapon and no witnesses.

And then, of course, there was Wallace Van Allen and his children. Van Allen's wife had died in an air crash in Paris three years before. The Van Allens, Reardon thought: prominent, wealthy, liberal, political. He looked up through the trees to their penthouse above.

When he reached Van Allen's building Reardon was astonished to find a familiar face. It was the doorman, Ben Steadman, an old detective who had retired six years earlier.

Politely, but with an initial, visible embarrassment, Steadman opened the door as Reardon approached.

"Hello, John," he said.

"Hello, Ben," Reardon replied, trying to conceal his own embarrassment.

"Who you looking for?"

"I'm supposed to see Wallace Van Allen this afternoon."

"You mean about the deer?" Steadman asked.

"Yeah."

"They transfer you out of homicide?"

"No," Reardon said, "they just wanted to put me on this one for a while."

"How come?"

"Because of Van Allen's money."

"Jesus, that's something, huh?"

"Did you see anything that night?" Reardon asked, in order to change from an uncomfortable subject.

Steadman smiled. "This an interrogation, Detective Reardon?"

"I just wondered."

"I told the boys who came over before. I had a bad night that night. Stomach trouble. Something I ate, probably. Anyway, I spent most of the morning on the toilet."

"Yeah," Reardon said, "but did you see anything at all that looked suspicious while you *were* out here?"

"Nothing, John," Steadman said, "and I've got a trained eye." He chuckled. "You never stop being a detective, you know."

Reardon smiled indulgently. "Well, which elevator do I take to Van Allen's apartment?"

"The penthouse has its own elevator," Steadman said. "I'll take you up."

Together they rode up in a mahogany-paneled

elevator. Reardon, glancing at Steadman's starched navy blue uniform with its shiny buttons and gilded brocade, saw his future possibilities and did not like them very much. He had hoped that he would be able to retire on a pension sufficient to his needs, at least if it could be augmented by the savings he and Millie had accumulated over the last thirty years, but Millie's medical bills had virtually devoured the savings.

When the elevator doors opened Reardon was ushered into the Van Allen apartment by a tall, middle-aged man who had the stiff, laconic manner of someone who had spent his life seeing to the trivial desires of others.

"Please sit down," he said. "Mr. Van Allen will be with you in a moment."

Reardon did not have to wait long, but while he waited his eyes roamed the room. It had the appearance of absolute stability, the confidence of its owners that they could deal with any conceivable distress.

"Detective Reardon?" someone said from behind him.

Reardon stood up. "Yes."

"Wallace Van Allen," said the tall man who had just entered the room. He looked younger than the photographs Reardon had seen of him in the newspapers. He was dressed in a black three-piece suit that looked as if it had never been worn before. He thrust out his hand energetically and Reardon politely shook it.

"I hear you're one crack cop," Mr. Van Allen said.

"Just an old cop."

"That's not what I hear," Mr. Van Allen said. "Please sit down, sit down."

Reardon sat back down on the sofa. Mr. Van Allen pulled up a chair facing him. "Terrible thing," he said, "just terrible." He looked at Reardon. "Psychopath, I suppose."

Reardon nodded. He had been examining Van Allen's face and had only barely heard his voice.

"The killer must be a psychopath," Mr. Van Allen repeated enthusiastically, emphasizing the word "killer." "What else could explain such an atrocious act? He must be mentally ill. No sane person could do such a thing. Don't you agree?"

"Maybe," Reardon said quietly.

"Well, I'm given to understand that if anyone can catch the poor fellow it is you."

"We don't have much to go on, right now."

"No one saw it, I suppose."

"Not that we know of."

Mr. Van Allen nodded his head sadly. "And no weapon either."

"How do you know?" Reardon asked.

Mr. Van Allen looked embarrassed. "I only assumed."

Reardon did not believe him. He suspected that the details of the case were being fed to Van Allen from high police officials downtown.

"Do you suppose the deer suffered much?" Mr. Van Allen asked.

A strange question, Reardon thought. "Did you see them?"

"Oh, no," Mr. Van Allen said. "I don't think I could. I suppose you know I donated those deer to the Children's Zoo in honor of my children's birthday. Beautiful animals. Very gentle. They were actually raised on our farm in the mountains. You should have seen them when they were young. So graceful, trotting about. I think they were my daughter's favorite things."

"How old is your daughter?" Reardon asked, without really knowing why.

"Sixteen."

"And your other children?"

"A son. Also sixteen. Why?"

"Just asking," Reardon said.

Mr. Van Allen leaned back in his seat, folding his hands tightly around the arms of his chair. He was suddenly staring at Reardon intently, almost fearfully, as a cautious, punctilious man might take in an unpredictable—and therefore frightening—event. It occurred to Reardon that this man had never experienced a policeman before. This adviser to mayors, senators and presidents had never descended into Reardon's soiled, awkward, accusing world, had never in his life been suspected—officially suspected—of anything.

Mr. Van Allen smiled and took a deep breath, but the anxiety was still in his eyes. "Yes," he said slowly, almost guardedly, "my children are twins. They're sixteen. They'll both be off to college next year. Very expensive, as I'm sure you know."

Reardon said nothing.

"Tell me," Mr. Van Allen said, "do you think we'll break this case?"

"I don't know," Reardon replied. Most of the time he did not know, could not know. "There are no weapons and no witnesses." There was no need to hold back information now. He suspected that at that moment Van Allen knew as much about the case as he did.

"I see," Mr. Van Allen said.

"Like I said, not much to go on."

"No, it appears that way."

Suddenly, Mr. Van Allen slapped his legs and stood up. Reardon recognized it as one of his son Timothy's new gestures. "Well," said Mr. Van Allen, "I just want to personally express my gratitude and the gratitude of my family for all you and your colleagues are doing for us and the Children's Zoo, and, I might add, for the City of New York."

It must have been a line he had said a thousand times, Reardon thought. It had been delivered like the concluding line of a campaign oration.

Reardon stood up. "Sure."

Mr. Van Allen thrust out his hand again and Reardon shook it.

"Thanks so much," Mr. Van Allen said.

Reardon nodded and moved toward the door.

"Poor fellow," Mr. Van Allen said wearily.

"Who?" Reardon asked quickly. For a moment he thought the "poor fellow" was himself.

"The guilty party. The man who harmed those innocent deer."

Reardon nodded once more and left the room the way he had come.

Outside he waited in a narrow hallway for the elevator. The walls were decked with portraits of bearded men in stern black suits and women in dresses with lace sleeves. Porcelain vases rested on the two tables standing on opposite sides of the room. Reardon could not guess how much the tables and vases must have cost, but standing near them made him nervous. He wondered if Timothy could stand in such a room without fear or self-consciousness, without being afraid that with any move or gesture he might send some irreplaceable artifact crashing down on the marble floor. He wondered if his son had come that far and lost that much, but, finally, he could not blame him if he had.

When the elevator door opened and Reardon stepped

into the car with Steadman, he felt as though as had been released from prison.

"Did you see Mr. Van Allen?" Steadman asked immediately.

Reardon nodded.

Steadman pushed a button and the elevator began its descent. "Nice place they got, huh? Did you see the aquarium they got?" Reardon noticed that there was some delight in his voice, as if it were his own aquarium.

"Nice people, the Van Allens," Steadman said, "real nice to everybody."

"Yeah."

When the penthouse elevator door opened Reardon found himself staring almost eye to eye with a young man who bore a striking resemblance to Wallace Van Allen. Reardon stepped aside, following Steadman into the lobby. Without a word, the young man leaped past him and into the elevator. Reardon turned for another look as the door closed.

"Who's that?" he asked Steadman.

"Dwight Van Allen, Mr. Van Allen's son."

"Where's his sister, the daughter?"

"She's a weird one," Steadman replied with visible caution. "She spends a lot of time in the park."

6

WEDNESDAY

The next morning Reardon looked up from his morning coffee in the precinct house to see an enormous man
looming over his desk. He looked like the sort of man
who never brought good news to anyone, whose complaints and irritabilities were always as exaggerated as
himself.

"Harry Bryant," the man said.

He was one of the largest men Reardon had ever
seen. His arms hung massively from his shoulders, and
each hand looked large enough to encircle a telephone
pole. Reardon quickly surmised that such a man could
easily sever the spine of a fallow deer with one blow.

"Sit down," Reardon said.

Bryant sat down, and for a moment Reardon wondered if the chair would support him.

"Want some coffee?" Reardon asked.

"Nope."

Reardon took a drink from his cup and examined
Bryant's face. He had light brown hair, balding at the
top. His eyes were blue and very watery, giving him
the appearance of being continually on the verge of
tears. He had a small mouth with a thin lower lip and
almost no upper lip at all. And there was something
beneath the face which Reardon could not touch upon

exactly—a kind of boiling honesty in large matters, coupled with heedless deviousness in small ones.

"I understand that you were on duty the morning the fallow deer were killed?" Reardon began.

"That's right." Bryant took a bent cigarette from his shirt pocket and lit it. "I was there." He threw his head back and blew a smoke ring.

Sometimes, Reardon knew, an unnatural nonchalance while being interrogated was as damning as a fingerprint. But he did not think this was the case with Bryant. Rather, he suspected that Bryant was utterly innocent, knew it, and felt confident in that knowledge.

"The deer were killed at approximately three-thirty A.M.," Reardon said. "Were you anywhere near the deer cage at around that time?"

Bryant looked at Reardon and smiled. "Can you keep a secret?"

"What do you mean?"

"I mean if I tell the Police Department something, do they have to blab to the Parks Department?"

"Depends on whether or not what you tell me is relevant to the case."

"Well, suppose a guy was guilty of goofing off, and that's all?"

"In that case, I would say that it has no relevance."

"What does that mean?"

"It means we can keep a secret."

"Well, in that case," Bryant said with a wink, "I was goofing off."

"That's okay," Reardon said. "Like I said, that has nothing to do with the case."

"I'm not the only slacker, you know. Hell, I bet you soak a little extra time out of the lunch hour, right?"

"Maybe." Reardon shifted in his chair, impatient with

Bryant's cheekiness. "While you were in the park did you see anything unusual?"

"Nope."

"Do you know of anyone who might have a grudge against the Parks Department?"

Bryant laughed. "Everybody who ever worked for that bunch of two-bit assholes has a grudge."

"Do you know of anybody who might take it out on the fallow deer?"

"Hell, no!" Bryant exclaimed. "And if I'd seen that son of a bitch, seen him hurting those deer, I'd have broken his goddamn neck! He'd of looked like those deer before I got through with him!"

"Noble talked about hearing something while he was working in the elephant cages," Reardon said. "A sound. Two sounds, really. A kind of harsh, grating sound and a kind of muffled one. Noble said it sounded like something being dragged."

Bryant took a handkerchief from his back pocket and swabbed his brow. "Noble says he heard something like that?"

"Yes. Around three or three-thirty, something like that."

"Oh, hell," Bryant said, "that explains why I didn't hear it. Like I said, I was goofing off."

"You were not in the zoo around that time?"

"No, I was in a coffee shop."

"Where?"

"On Second Avenue, over from the park. All-night place there. But, you know, you might ask Andros. He was on his way to the zoo around that time."

"Who was?"

"Andros," Bryant said. "You know, Petrakis."

"The other workman?"

"Yeah."

"I thought he was out sick."

"Well, he was in a way," Bryant said. "He called in sick on Sunday afternoon, I understand. But I saw him walking by the coffee shop at about three A.M. Maybe a little before." Bryant stubbed his cigarette out in the ashtray. "Anyway, I called him in. He came in for just a minute, wouldn't sit down. He's been real upset lately on account of his wife's been sick and he's been thrown out of his apartment."

"He was evicted?"

"Yeah, him and his whole goddamn family. I guess he couldn't pay the rent because of the medical bills."

"So the landlord evicted him?"

"That's right," Bryant said. "Wouldn't you if you was his landlord?"

Reardon avoided asking himself that question. "But he came to work that night?"

"Yeah. He said he'd been busy with his kids, you know. The wife's been sick and so he had to do all the work in the house."

"And you say he was upset?"

"Yeah," Bryant said, "upset and mad as hell."

"Who was he mad at?"

"The landlord, who else?"

Reardon nodded.

"He was really pissed, you know what I mean?" Bryant said. "He didn't know what he was going to do. He looked like he was about ready to give up on everything. He borrowed ten bucks from me, and he's never done that before. I never seen him ask anybody on the job for a penny. But he was broke. I mean *broke*. So I gave him a ten spot. We was kind of friendly on the job, you know? We used to take our breaks together.

We always used to go to this little coffee shop, the one I told you about, the one on Second Avenue."

"Did you see where he went when he left the coffee shop?"

"Yeah, he walked out in the direction of the zoo."

"You sure?"

"Yeah. He crossed the street going toward the zoo, up Sixty-fourth Street," Bryant said. "The coffee shop is right on the corner of Sixty-fourth Street and Second Avenue. I could see him for a good ways. He was walking toward the park."

"Why did he decide to come to work?"

"Needed the money," Bryant said. "Why do you decide to come to work?" He looked mockingly at Reardon. "He ran out of vacation time and sick time and all that, but they been letting him kind of work by the hour, you know?"

"What time did he leave the coffee shop?" Reardon asked.

"I don't know for sure. About three A.M. or so, I guess."

"How long were you in the coffee shop?"

"Too long. I should have been doing the aviary at about three."

"Why weren't you?"

"Have you ever owned a bird?"

"No," Reardon said.

"Well, if you had you'd know they shit all the time, and when you got ten or fifteen birds in a cage, that cage is going to be covered with bird shit no matter how much you clean it. So I decided I'd stay a few extra minutes in the coffee shop and then just hose it down when I got back. That don't take long."

"How long were you in the coffee shop?"

"Hell, I must have been there for about an hour and a half, from a little before three till about four-thirty."

"What were you doing before you left the zoo?"

"Well, for a while me and Gil was working on some of them monkey cages. Then Gil went to do the elephant cages." Bryant winked. "He already had his break, you know?"

Reardon nodded.

"From about one to two-thirty," Bryant added impishly.

"That doesn't matter."

"Maybe not to you, but to the Parks Department it matters, by God. They'd raise holy shit if they knew."

"Uh huh," Reardon sighed, no longer able to conceal his total indifference.

"Poor old Petrakis," Bryant said. "He should have stayed out one more night."

"Why?" Reardon asked.

"Because I understand his wife died that night."

Reardon spent the rest of the day trying to get in touch with Andros Petrakis. He found the entire Petrakis story suspicious.

During the early afternoon Reardon called the Petrakis home twenty-three times. There was no answer. The Parks Department informed Reardon that they had not heard from Petrakis since the Monday morning following the killings. At nine A.M. on Monday he had called to tell Mr. Raymond Cohen, his superior in the Parks Department, that his wife had died during the night and that he would not be back to work until the following Monday. The deteriorating condition of Mrs. Petrakis had been well known to Mr. Cohen, and consequently he had not associated the phone call and week's ab-

sence with the slaughter that had taken place in the
cage of the fallow deer during the early morning hours
of that same day. It was noticed, however, that Petrakis had made his call from a pay phone booth. Petrakis
had rambled somewhat in the conversation, using up
the time allotted for a pay phone call, and had been
interrupted by a recording warning him to terminate
the conversation or deposit additional money. At that
point, according to Mr. Cohen, Petrakis had quickly
finished his conversation and hung up.

Next Reardon called Harry Bryant to see if he had
heard from Petrakis. He had not. Petrakis had not
spoken to Bryant since the meeting in the coffee shop.

"But I got the feeling you two were friendly," Reardon said.

"Well, we were in a way," Bryant said, "but Andros
was a kind of close-knit ethnic type. I got the feeling
all his friends were Greek." Bryant did not know any
of Petrakis' Greek friends.

After speaking to Bryant, Reardon told Mathesson to
find out who owned the building from which Petrakis
had been evicted. Then he decided to visit the building
himself.

Until the eviction Petrakis and his family had lived
at the top of a five-floor walk-up on 90th Street and
First Avenue. It was a dirty, steaming tenement, not
much different from thousands of others in the city. As
he gazed up toward the fifth-floor windows Reardon
could not imagine being evicted from such a place,
being forcefully excluded from a rat hole like this.
Where could a man and his family go, he thought, if
they were already at the bottom?

He opened the door into the hallway that led to the
stairs, and the warm, almost sweet smell of urine en-

veloped him. The hallway was full of debris: a partially
burned mattress, beer cans, a disemboweled television,
the bare, rusty, wheel-less skeleton of a bicycle. The
walls were covered with a dark, murky layer of mold,
and the squeaking stairs were littered with the plaster
that had fallen from the walls and ceiling overhead.
As Reardon made his way toward the fifth floor he
could hear the easy frolicking of rats.

When he reached the Petrakis apartment Reardon
knocked lightly on the door, then listened for movement inside the apartment. There was only silence. He
knocked again, harder this time, but still there was no
response. He turned to the door facing the Petrakis
apartment and knocked. Inside he could hear rustling,
hurried movement, but the door did not open to him.

He knocked again.

"Yes?" a voice said, but still the door did not open.

"My name is Detective John Reardon, Police Department. I'm looking for Andros Petrakis."

"Moved," the voice said. Reardon could tell that it
was the voice of an old man. Each word was preceded
and followed by a wheeze.

"Yes, I know," Reardon said, "but we can't get in
touch with him. We were wondering if anyone in this
building might know where the Petrakis family moved
after they left the building."

"Took his family," the voice said.

"Yes, I know."

"Sick wife. Lots of kids."

"Yes, I know," Reardon said. He did not ask the old
man to open the door. He knew that he would not. He
did not even want to frighten him by asking. "But do
you know any of Mr. Petrakis' friends? Did he have
any friends in this building, anyone who visited him?"

"Don't know," the voice said through a gentle

cough. "Don't know nothing about them. Just lots of kids."

"I'm sorry to have troubled you," Reardon said, giving in, and he touched the door, gently with his fingertips, as he might have soothed a troubled face.

7

That night, as Reardon slept, two women were murdered in an apartment on Fifth Avenue and 12th Street, a fashionable area in the center of Greenwich Village. When Smith informed Reardon of the crime the next morning he described it as a "bloody" and told Reardon that Piccolini wanted to talk to him.

"Have you read the report on the murder of those two girls in the Village?" Piccolini asked. To Piccolini all females were girls, no matter what their age.

"How old were they?" Reardon asked.

"Twenties. It's all in the report. You didn't read it yet, huh?"

"No."

"Well, it's all in there. In the report. It's on your desk."

"I haven't been to my desk."

Piccolini looked irritated. Reardon knew that not going to the desk first thing struck Piccolini as being symptomatic of a serious social maladjustment. "Well, anyway, Mathesson was over there this morning, and there are some strange things about it. It might be a good idea for you to take a look. Like there's a number scrawled on the wall of their apartment, and it's the same number."

"Two?" Reardon asked.

"Yes."

Reardon felt a wave of tension pass over his body. "A roman numeral?"

"No, it's in Spanish. Dos. And it's written in blood."

"What was the weapon?"

"Probably some kind of broad-bladed knife. And another thing: one of them was hacked up real bad, and the other one was killed with one blow. Just one. That's it."

"Do you have a pathologist's report?"

"No. The bodies are still at the apartment." Piccolini looked pleadingly at Reardon. "Look, why don't you just go over there. Just go on over there. You'll get more there than out of me. Talk to Mathesson about the details. He's been there since early this morning."

Reardon nodded.

"All I'm saying is that we maybe have more than a deer killer on our hands. So if by chance you've been feeling deprived of your homicide cases, well, now you've got one. If it turns out there's no connection between the two cases that's okay, but the burden of proof has to go against the connection."

With Piccolini Reardon could never tell whether phrases like "burden of proof" came from reading or television. "I'll let you know what I find," he said.

At the apartment of the murdered women Reardon found the usual swarm of investigators. They were dusting for fingerprints and photographing the bodies from every conceivable angle. A group of uniformed officers stood in corners chatting about baseball scores or comparing arrest records, but otherwise the room was a welter of activity. Mathesson stood near the center of the room writing in his notebook.

"It doesn't look like they were sexually abused," he said as Reardon approached him.

Reardon scanned the apartment. It looked as if it had been blown up with a hand grenade. Everything was in disarray—overturned, scattered, bloodied. "They look like they were pretty abused without it."

"We think they died sometime between midnight and five in the morning," Mathesson said. "We can't get much closer than that right now. We're checking everybody in the building, trying to find out when they got home."

"Who were they?" Reardon asked.

"Two women, roommates. Both names are on the mailboxes downstairs. One of them is named Lee McDonald, and the other one—the one in the other room—is named Karen Ortovsky."

"Anything else?"

"McDonald worked at a law firm. The other one worked for some fashion place. A designer, maybe. Something like that." Mathesson's face turned ruminative. "But there's something kind of funny."

"What's that?"

"Well, we haven't been able to find any address book or anything like that around here. There's a lot of cash. Fifty-five dollars in this little desk, another seventy-five in the kitchen, and a hundred and twenty bucks in a nightstand in the other room. But no address book at all. No file of telephone numbers. No list of friends. Nothing like that. It don't seem quite right, to tell you the truth. I mean, hell, every woman has a list of names and telephone numbers."

Reardon peered around the room. "Did you check the back of the phone book?"

"Yeah. Nothing. Blank. No names written in it or circled anywhere in the book. He looked for some response in Reardon's face, then he added: "A couple of boys are going through all the clothes in the bedroom, but so far we just got the stuff in their purses, you know. Company ID's and credit cards. That sort of shit."

Reardon took out his notebook. "Give me the names of the companies they worked for."

Mathesson took out his notebook and quickly thumbed through it until he reached the correct page. "McDonald worked for a law firm named Bailey, Merritt and White. They're at 1604 Sixth Avenue. The other one worked at Tristan Designers at 147 West 37th Street."

"Okay. And find out which bank they used and check out any safety deposit boxes they might have had. There might be something in them we ought to know about. And keep looking for some kind of address book. I don't see any signs of a forced entry here so they may have known the killer, may have had his name written down somewhere."

"Yeah," Mathesson said, "like I said, that might explain why they're missing names and numbers."

"Maybe," Reardon said.

"Well, I guess you want to look around."

"Yeah."

"The other one's tied up in the bedroom closet," Mathesson said.

Reardon nodded. He took a deep breath, exhaled quickly, nervously, stepped past Mathesson and walked farther into the apartment. He did not like what he saw.

Lee McDonald lay near the far wall, opposite the apartment entrance. She had been butchered like a hog on a rack, stabbed in both eyes, her throat cut almost to the spinal column. There were deep slashes in both her thighs and one long deep cut across her left jaw. One breast had been almost severed from her body and hung like a flap over her rib cage. The other breast had been flayed open by numerous thrusts of the blade. She had been stabbed completely through one hand, splitting it in two between the middle and index fingers.

"All her clothes were just cut off her," Mathesson said as he stepped up behind Reardon. "Like opening a package."

Slithers of clothing lay scattered about the room like discarded ribbons. All the furniture on the right side of the room—two small chairs and a table—was overturned; one of the chairs had been thrown all the way to the other side of the room and rested on its side near Lee McDonald's ankles. On the back wall a painting was tipped far to the right, and the small pink sofa that rested below it was dappled with blood. The left wall of the room was covered with blood, but none of the furniture was disturbed.

From the position of the body and its condition, and from the splotches on the walls, Reardon could visualize what must have happened in that room during the last two or three minutes of Lee McDonald's life.

Someone had come through the front and only door of the apartment. He had had with him—under his coat or wrapped like a package or hidden in a newspaper—a broad-bladed knife, perhaps ten to twelve inches long and three to five inches wide at its greatest width. With this weapon, and perhaps some other one —even a gun—he had forced both women into the adjoining bedroom, where he had tied up Karen Ortovsky and dumped her in the bedroom closet like a bag of dirty laundry.

Then he must have told Lee to come with him into the living room. Either that, or she had attempted flight, tried to make it to the only door. But too late.

"Where's the other woman?" Reardon asked.

Mathesson pointed to the open bedroom door. "In there."

Reardon nodded and went into the bedroom.

In the brutal relativity of murder, Karen Ortovsky had gotten off easier. Her body lay in the bedroom closet adjoining the room in which Lee McDonald had died. She was bound and gagged, her legs bent under her at the knees and tied at the ankles. Her throat had been cut almost to the spinal column. Her eyes were wide open and a piece of tissue paper, part of the gag that had been crammed all the way to the windpipe, dangled ludicrously from the left side of her mouth.

Reardon stared at the face. It was an ordinary face. But it suddenly appeared to him to be the smallest, most delicately etched and hideously violated face he had ever seen on an adult. With its up-turned nose and small, thin mouth, barely wider than a half-dollar piece, it seemed to retain the features of a child.

Reardon knelt down beside the slumped body of Karen Ortovsky and with two fingers gently closed her eyes.

"Well, what do you think?" Mathesson asked as he walked into the bedroom. "Do you think there's a connection with the deer thing?"

Reardon stood up slowly, feeling a weakness in his knees. "I don't know."

"Piccolini thinks there is, right?"

"Yeah." He looked down again into the face of the body crumpled at his feet. "Sometimes enough is enough," he whispered.

"Huh?"

Somehow, Reardon thought, if the eyes had been closed, like those of Lee McDonald, he could have borne the rest with greater ease. But the eyes of Karen Ortovsky had burned into him like naked light bulbs in a solid darkness, screaming for more than conventional justice could offer. Reardon knew immediately that Karen Ortovsky had been the last to die. He knew that she had cowered, tied like a beast, while the murderous tumult went on in the next room. She had heard each slash of the blade tearing into Lee McDonald's flesh, had heard her roommate's body pivot and stagger into tables, overturn chairs, flail wildly against each wall and then finally collapse helplessly to the floor, where only the final whimpering exhalations could be heard above the merciless whirring of the blade.

Reardon shuddered and quickly walked out into the other room.

"So now you're back in homicide," Reardon heard Mathesson say behind him, but he could not answer. "I knew you would be. I knew it was coming. Just like I said that day at the zoo, about those deer. It's the same thing. Just like the guy with the cats. A maniac like that will eventually get around to people. It never fails. I've never seen it to fail."

Reardon stood in the middle of the living room, as silent and immobile as an icon. "She seemed so small," he said.

"Yeah," Mathesson replied, "that little McDonald girl couldn't of been more than five feet tall."

"I meant Karen," Reardon said. "Her face was so small, like a child's face."

"I didn't notice, to tell you the truth." Mathesson took a cigarette from his pocket and lit it. "But I knew it would come to people in the end. It always does. Just like that scumbag with the cats."

Reardon shook his head. He turned toward the entrance of the apartment. "I've got to step out for some fresh air," he said to Mathesson. "It's stifling in here."

He went out and down the stairs and outside into the

street. Images came whirling into his mind: Van Allen. The dead fallow deer. Millie. Piccolini. Tim. Finally Karen Ortovsky. He walked a few yards down the street and leaned for support against a parking meter. The meter was cold but he could not let go of it. Over and over his mind kept returning to three phases from his abandoned religion. They seemed to circle in his mind like vultures in a desert sky. They were the last words of excommunication: Ring the bell. Close the book. Quench the candle.

8

Later in the morning Reardon joined Mathesson in a canvass of the building in which Lee McDonald and Karen Ortovsky had been murdered. It was a five-floor walk-up and the two women had lived on the third floor. It had no doorman. Mathesson took the two floors above the third floor; Reardon took the two below it, beginning on the first floor.

There were two apartments on each landing. Reardon knocked several times at one apartment, but there was no answer. He walked across the hall to the other apartment and knocked on the door there. He waited a moment, then knocked again. After another pause the door opened slightly.

"Yes?" a voice inquired.

Reardon could see half a face peering between the two separate lengths of chain that held the door secure. "My name is Reardon," he said, "New York City Police. I'd like to talk with you a minute." He took out his shield and presented it.

"Oh, fine," the voice said with obvious relief.

Reardon watched as the chains were undone and the door swung open to allow him in.

The man inside was short and very fat. His head was completely bald, but his face was covered with a massive black beard. Still, Reardon thought, it was an

expressive face, mobile, the eyes darting about con-
stanly like two blue marbles on a roulette wheel.

The man thrust out his hand. "My name is John
Levinson," he said. He smiled broadly. "Always happy
to help the police. Never know when you might need
a cop, you know."

Reardon shook the outstretched hand. "John Reardon," he said quietly. Such overt friendliness turned
Reardon toward a shy, withdrawn self-consciousness.

"Have a seat," Levinson said, pointing to a wicker
chair. "Right there's fine."

Reardon sat down. "Thanks."

Levinson sat down on a small sofa opposite Reardon
and folded his arms across his chest. He looked, to
Reardon, like one of those big-bellied Buddhas he had
seen displayed in Village novelty shops.

"What can I do for you?" Levinson asked.

"I don't know if you're aware of it, but we had two
murders in this building last night."

Levinson covered his mouth with his hand. "My
God!" he muttered through his fingers. "Who?"

"Two women on the third floor named Lee Mc-
Donald and Karen Ortovsky. Did you know them?"

Levinson shook his head. "No. How were they
killed?"

"I can't go into the details," Reardon replied.

Levinson nodded. "Brutal?"

"It wasn't pretty."

"Hm," Levinson said. "Career girls probably, right?"

"They had jobs," Reardon said, growing uncomfortable with the style of Levinson's interest.

Levinson suddenly shot out of his chair and went to
a bookcase. His eyes moved across one of the shelves
until he found what he was looking for. He took a

paperback book from the shelf and looked at the cover. "Five hundred thousand copies sold," he muttered to himself. Then he returned the book to the shelf and sat back down across from Reardon. "That's really something," he said, staring at Reardon. "Two white career girls brutally murdered in an exclusive Village brownstone." He stroked his beard again. "Yeah, that could be something. There could be a book in there. That could really be something. Did you say they lived on the third floor?"

"Yeah."

Levinson slapped his thigh. "Well, I'll be damned," he said enthusiastically. "Now that you mention it. Two girls on the third floor. I used to see them getting their mail out there in the foyer. Yeah, I used to see them. They were both lookers. Good lookers. Probably photographed well."

"When was the last time you saw them?" Reardon asked.

"Oh, I don't know," Levinson said casually. "Several days ago, I guess."

"Did you ever see them with anybody else?"

"No. No. I don't think so."

Reardon stood up. "I guess that's it, then."

Levinson jumped to his feet. "Just a second, Mr. Reardon," he said, his eyes darting about the apartment. "How about a drink? I got some high-class stuff."

"No, thanks." Reardon said, starting toward the door.

Levinson grabbed Reardon's arm. "Uh, wait a minute. I, uh, I might have a proposition to make to you."

Reardon stopped and Levinson released Reardon's

arm. "Look," he said nervously, "I'm a writer. You
know? Free-lance. This sounds to me like it could be
a real story. A big story. Maybe we could work together on it."

"This is a murder investigation," Reardon replied
coolly.

"I know, I know, but these things make a good
read. There's a big audience for this sort of thing."

"I'm a homicide detective," Reardon said. He could
not think of any other reply.

"Yeah," Levinson said enthusiastically, "that's great!
You got all the dope! You got the inside track! You've
seen the bodies, that sort of thing! You got access to
pictures!"

Reardon could feel the heat rising in his face. "Go
fuck yourself," he said.

Levinson stepped back. "So who are you, Rocke-
feller?" he snapped.

Reardon opened the door of the apartment and
stepped into the hall.

"You think that's the end of it, don't you?" Levinson
shouted after him.

Reardon did not respond. He proceeded down the
hallway toward the stairs.

"Well, it's not. It's not the end of it," Levinson
called. "I'll get it from somebody else. You think you're
the only flatfoot in this fucking shit-hole town?"

Reardon did not turn around. He started up the
stairs to the second floor.

On the second floor Reardon found one empty, un-
rented apartment and one witness.

The witness was a small-framed middle-aged woman
with thick tortoise-shell glasses. As she opened the

door to let him enter, Reardon noticed that she wore a flimsy nightgown that was almost transparent.

The living room was painted bright red with yellow trim. B-movie posters were plastered to the walls in various places, and a picture of Florenz Ziegfeld was illuminated by a fluorescent bulb.

"My mother's," the woman explained. "She always claimed to be his mistress." She stared at the picture contemptuously. "She was full of crap. To the day she died, just full of crap." She turned to Reardon and smiled. "Sit down," she said. "Rest your feet."

Reardon sat down. The woman slid into the chair opposite him with an exaggerated gesture of grace.

"I'm Mrs. Marjorie Malloy, but you can call me Meg."

"How long have you lived in this apartment, Mrs. Malloy?" Reardon asked.

"Longer than it takes to spit, by God," she replied with a grin. "Thirty-two years."

"You know there was a double murder in this building last night?"

"I figured something like that. Place was blue as a strangled nun with all you cops this morning."

Reardon shook his head to dissolve the repellent image. "The victims were the two women who live upstairs. Lee McDonald and Karen Ortovsky. Did you know them?"

"Just to say hi in the hall."

"When did you see them last?"

"This morning, about three A.M. That was funny, too," Mrs. Malloy added. "They usually kept regular hours." She smiled. "They was lezzies, you know."

"The two women?"

"Yep." Mrs. Malloy looked at Reardon suggestively. "I'm a man's woman, myself."

"Did you stay home the rest of the night?"

"Naw, I went right back out again. Like I said, I'm a man's woman. I met this guy in the bar, Donahue's down the street, and we got to talking and he invited me over to his house, you know? So I told him okay, but I needed to get some things from my place. So he wanted to come with me, but I says, 'Hell, no,' I says, 'I live in a high-class building, so I have to keep a low profile,' you know?"

Reardon nodded.

"These assholes in this building will complain about anything, so you have to watch yourself. I been a widow for longer than I can remember. No children. I can have my fun, but I keep it private."

"When you saw them this morning, were they alone?"

"No, they had somebody with them."

"Can you describe that person?"

"Kind of tall. About six feet, I guess. But if she was a he, then he was kind of average size, I guess." She hesitated. "You see, they all had their backs to me. The other one was walking in between Karen and Lee, and they were all wearing jeans and shirts and that person had long black hair. So I couldn't tell if it was male or female."

Reardon stared down at his pen as it scratched across his notebook.

"You've got a sensitive look," Mrs. Malloy said.

Reardon did not look up.

"Sensitive eyes. Sensitive hands and face. What else is sensitive?"

Reardon looked up. He repeated his previous question. "Did you know either Miss McDonald or Miss Ortovsky very well?"

"Not very. They was lezzies, and I'm not. I stay the hell away from that sort."

"How did you know that?" Reardon asked.

Mrs. Malloy laughed. "I could hear them going at each other at night. Moaning and groaning, you know. Sometimes I'd see them bring a man up to their rooms. But that didn't mean nothing. In just a little while I could hear them going at each other again." She laughed. Don't get me wrong. I don't give a damn. Kicks is kicks, but I get my kicks from a man."

Reardon stood up. "I guess that's it for now."

Mrs. Malloy walked him to the door and opened it. "Don't get me wrong," she said softly, "I'm sorry about those girls."

"I know," Reardon replied.

"I hope I didn't embarrass you. I sometimes embarrass people." She paused a moment, glanced down at her feet, then up to Reardon's face. "I sometimes embarrass myself," she added wearily.

Reardon put out his hand and Mrs. Malloy took it in hers.

"Thank you for coming forward, Mrs. Malloy."

She smiled faintly, sadly, "It's my duty, right?"

"Yeah, it is," Reardon said.

Reardon spent the rest of the day in the Buildings Department. He hoped that Petrakis' former landlord might know where he had moved, but the apartment house from which he had been evicted was owned by the Upward Real Estate Company, which was, in turn, owned by the Amalgamated Owners Cooperative. Methodically Reardon pursued this corporation, only to discover that it was held by yet another: the East

Coast Realty Investors Company. East Coast was a subsidiary of an even larger real estate corporation called the New York Investment Enterprise, Inc.

And for all intents and purposes, New York Investment was owned and controlled by a single individual: Wallace Van Allen.

9

FRIDAY

On Friday morning Reardon reported to Piccolini on the fallow deer and the murdered women. He began with the deer. "Bryant said—"

"Now that's the guy that works with Petrakis, right?" Piccolini interrupted.

"That's right. He said that he saw Petrakis about three A.M. in a coffee shop only a few blocks from the zoo. Petrakis told him that he was just about broke and that he had decided to come to work that night because he needed the money."

"Okay," Piccolini said.

"But Petrakis never reported coming to work that night to anybody in the Parks Department."

Piccolini nodded.

Reardon continued. "Now Bryant said that Petrakis was in a rage at being thrown out of his old apartment on the East Side. He kept talking about how rotten his landlord was, how he hated him, all that."

"So?"

"Well, his landlord was Wallace Van Allen," Reardon said. "It's our first real angle. Our first connection. It may not be anything, not even worth a second thought, but it could be something. Petrakis could have killed the deer to get back at Van Allen."

"For evicting him."

"Right."

"He knew that Van Allen gave the deer to the zoo?" Piccolini asked.

"All the people at the zoo knew that and Petrakis was working at the zoo when the donation was made. It's not likely that he wouldn't have been aware of it. You know all the publicity it got."

"Yeah," Piccolini agreed, "he would have to have known. Where is this Petrakis?"

"We haven't been able to locate him yet. After he was evicted nobody seems to know where he went."

"Well, find him," Piccolini said. "And do it fast. I would be the last person to blame it on the guy if there's no connection, but he could be our man."

"And we've also got a cocaine bust not far from where the deer were killed at about the same time—I mean, a little after the time they were killed. We're trying to get to talk to the guy who got busted."

"Trying to talk to him? What's the problem?"

"Well, there's a lot of lawyers between him and us."

The idea of a lot of smart lawyers hanging around a potential witness seemed to cool Piccolini's determination. "Well, do your best," he said quietly. Then he changed the subject. "What about the girls in the Village?"

"We have one witness."

Piccolini's ears perked up like those of a hunting dog. "A witness?"

"Well, not to the murders themselves . . ." Reardon added quickly. "Not a witness to those. But a woman saw the women go up to the apartment with a third person."

"Description?"

"No. They all had their backs turned the whole time. They were going up the stairs."

Piccolini nodded. "Well, what about that number? Dos?"

"It's there. Probably written in Lee McDonald's blood."

"How'd the bodies look?" Piccolini asked. Then he caught himself. "I don't mean exactly how. But I mean, was what Mathesson said right? Was one of them pretty well cut up and the other one not?"

"Yeah," Reardon said. He did not want to go any further with it, any more than Piccolini wanted him to.

"Well, is that it, then?"

"For now it is," Reardon said.

"Okay," Piccolini said. "Stay busy."

Reardon nodded and walked out of the office. Yeah, he thought, stay busy.

Late that afternoon Reardon met Melinda Van Allen in the Children's Zoo. He had remembered Steadman saying that she was a strange girl and that she spent a lot of time in the park. It was not altogether inconceivable, Reardon thought, that she could have killed the fallow deer. Cases had been broken on slimmer leads before. Consequently he had gone back to Van Allen's building and mentioned to Steadman that he wanted to question Melinda Van Allen. Steadman had told him she was not in the building, but that he could probably find her sitting in the Children's Zoo.

That was where he found her.

"Miss Van Allen?" he said as he approached.

She looked up from a book. "Yes?"

Reardon had expected her to be prettier than she was. He had never really discarded the notion that rich young women were always beautiful. But Melinda Van Allen was not. She was large-boned and slightly overweight. Her hair was coarse and unruly, and her face was plain except for a certain fragile softness about the eyes which Reardon—in his present state of mind —instantly took to be a sign of sadness.

"My name is John Reàrdon. I'm a detective with the New York City Police Department. I'm investigating the killing of the deer your father donated to the zoo." He sat down on the bench beside her. "It's a pleasant day, isn't it?"

"Lovely," Melinda said. "Would you like some grapes?" She held out a paper bag.

"No, thank you."

"Now that the boycott is over, I can eat all I want," she said.

Reardon nodded. During the strike in the California vineyards he had quietly boycotted grapes himself.

"I'm very sorry about the deer," Melinda said.

"Do you come to the zoo often?"

"All the time. It's one of my favorite places. I wanted to be a veterinarian when I was a child."

Reardon smiled. He shoved his hands into his overcoat pockets to protect them from the cold. He noticed that Melinda did not seem to be bothered much by the chill that surrounded them. But her coat was much heavier than his and, of course, she was younger.

"I wanted to be a kind of female Saint Francis," Melinda explained.

"Is that what you're studying in school," Reardon asked, "veterinary medicine?"

Melinda frowned. "Oh, no, that was just a childhood thing. No, I'm studying art now. I want to be a sculptress. There's no money in it of course."

That struck Reardon as a curious remark from such a rich young woman, but he kept his opinion to himself.

"But I love it, you see," she said energetically. "It's

a passion with me." She looked intently into Reardon's face. "I think it is important to be passionately committed to your work, don't you, Mr. Reardon?"

"I suppose," Reardon said. "Of course, some jobs don't call for much passion."

"But all jobs should," Melinda said very seriously. "No one should do anything without having a total commitment to it. Total commitment is the key. Don't you think? Total commitment is the necessary element of total happiness. Without it, there is only frustration and bitterness."

Reardon felt reasonably certain that Melinda had underlined and memorized that remark from something she had read. "Maybe so," he said.

"Have you ever read Carlos Castenada?" she asked.

"Who?"

"Carlos Castenada. He's a sociologist."

"No."

"Well, he had a great experience with Don Juan, an old Indian. And Don Juan says that there are many roads down which a man may travel, but only one of them has a heart."

Reardon did not know what that meant. "Do you know of anyone who might have wanted to hurt the fallow deer?"

Melinda lowered her head. "No," she whispered.

"Any people mad at you or your brother or your father or anything like that?"

"No," Melinda said. "I don't think any of us have any enemies."

Reardon could not imagine that being true. "Almost everyone makes somebody mad at them sometime," he said.

Melinda did not reply. She popped a single grape into her mouth and began to munch it quietly.

"Miss Van Allen," Reardon said sternly, "we are dealing with someone capable of a more serious crime than the killing of animals."

Melinda turned toward him furiously. "What could be more serious than that?" she demanded.

Reardon was jolted by the question. He looked deeply into Melinda's face to assure himself that she was serious, and saw that she was. "The killing of human beings," he said.

"Human beings are only animals," Melinda said, "and animals are just as sensitive as human beings, just as capable of feeling pain and loss. Do you eat meat?"

"Yes," Reardon said, almost defensively.

Melinda smirked. "Well, then. You're a killer."

Reardon could feel himself growing angry. "Miss Van Allen, I am trying to solve a crime. Someone killed those deer, and whoever it was may have also killed two young women. Two women not much older than yourself."

"I can't help you," Melinda shot back.

Reardon stood up. "No," he said, "I don't suppose you can."

As he was about to walk away, Melinda grabbed his hand. "Sit down a minute," she said.

"Why?" The fierceness with which she held his hand suggested to Reardon that she might have something important on her mind. He did not try to pull away.

"Please," she said.

Reardon sat down again beside her and watched carefully as her face relaxed. It was as if she were using her face, positioning it for maximum effect. Everything around her—the cold, the gray sidewalk lined on either side by strips of dead brown grass, the black-lacquered bars of the animal cages—everything seemed to accentuate Melinda's face, and as Reardon peered at it, waited for her to speak, it seemed the only thing in the park that was really alive.

"How do you feel right now?" Melinda asked. "Inside, in your emotions, right this second?"

"Miss Van Allen, I am trying to find a person who is killing things, animals and maybe people."

Melinda smiled sweetly. "I know that," she said, "but how do you feel, right now, right this second?"

Reardon paused. She was staring at him intently, fixedly, and it came out before he could stop himself. "Alone," he said.

"Why?"

Reardon felt ridiculous, but he answered her anyway. "Well, for one thing, my wife died recently."

"Are you mourning her?"

"Naturally."

"Have you ever read much Buddhist philosophy?"

Reardon was growing impatient, regretting that he had mentioned Millie's death. Such things, things like mourning, he had always considered to be very private, no one else's business. "No," he said.

"Oh, you should!" Melinda exclaimed excitedly. "There is a story in Buddhist philosophy about a woman who lost her husband to death, and she just could not stop mourning for him. She was simply incapacitated by her grief. She went to see the Buddha, and the Buddha said for her to make a potion out of a few very common herbs. But he said that the herbs must be gathered from households in which no one had ever died, in which there had never been a death."

Reardon nodded.

"Well, the woman could not find a single household where there had not been a death."

Reardon looked at Melinda blankly.

"Well, don't you see?" she said. "The woman learned that everyone has grief, everyone experiences the death of loved ones, relatives and husbands; but everyone learns to bear it. And so could she."

Reardon stood up and handed Melinda his card. "If you come upon any information that might help me in finding the person who killed the deer, call me."

"But don't you see?" Melinda asked, almost pleadingly.

"Keep that card," Reardon said, and he turned and walked away.

When he reached the street above the zoo, the story of the Buddha was still on Reardon's mind. But he could not understand how the knowledge that everyone suffers could possibly ease the suffering of anyone.

10

"We can't find a goddamn thing," Mathesson told Reardon as he walked through the doors of the precinct house. "We've searched that apartment like a swarm of bees looking for honey and there's not an address to be found anywhere."

"Did you check the phone book again?" Reardon asked.

"Yeah. Nothing. Absolutely nothing. It's like those two girls were found in a hotel room on another planet. It's like they just got into New York the night they got wasted and didn't know anybody, not a single person in the whole city."

Reardon turned back toward the doors to the street.

"Where are you going?" Mathesson asked.

"I'm going to check out where they worked."

"You want some company?"

Reardon could see that Mathesson was looking at him worriedly, appraising him, trying to determine if he was still fit enough to be a homicide detective. "No," he replied, "you go ahead with your other cases. I'll handle it."

Tristan Designers looked to Reardon like a chic setup. The walls of the foyer were covered with mahogany paneling, and everything else looked as if it was either plated with gold or upholstered in silk. .

"May I help you, sir?" the receptionist asked, and

111

it was clear from the abrupt tone of her voice that Reardon did not resemble anyone she thought might have serious, legitimate business there.

He took out his detective's shield. "My name is John Reardon. I'm investigating the murder of one of your employees. I'd like to talk to whoever supervised Miss Ortovsky."

"That would be Helene Pynchon," the receptionist said. "You'd like to talk with her now?"

Reardon gazed patiently at the receptionist. "Well, two women have been murdered," he said.

"Yes. Yes, of course," the receptionist said. "Just a moment, please. Please have a seat over there. I'll call Miss Pynchon right away." She sounded to Reardon a lot like his son's secretary, a person who spent her life protecting somebody who wouldn't use the same toilet she did.

When Helene Pynchon walked out into the foyer her appearance did not surprise Reardon. She was tall and dark-haired with thin, pale arms. She was dressed in a loose-fitting pastel blouse and a long skirt. Reardon guessed her age at approximately forty-five. She looked like hundreds of other women Reardon had seen and faintly desired as they walked along Park Avenue or Central Park West.

"Good afternoon," she said pleasantly as Reardon rose from his chair. "I'm Helene Pynchon."

"My name is Reardon. I'm investigating the murders of Karen Ortovsky and her roommate. Is there some-place we could talk?"

"Of course. Come into my office, won't you."

In her office Miss Pynchon offered Reardon a chair and seated herself behind the desk.

"Now," she said, "how can I help? We were so upset

when we found out about Karen this morning. Her death, I mean."

"Did you know her very well?"

"Not very. Only professionally. She did excellent work at Tristan."

"Did you ever see her socially?"

"No. Never. It was purely a professional association. I make it a point never to have personal relationships with anyone on my staff."

Reardon nodded. He didn't go out with the mayor much either. "How about anybody else on your staff?" he asked. "Did she have any close friends here?"

Miss Pynchon thought for a moment. "I believe she and Laura Murray had a nonprofessional relationship."

"Nonprofessional? You mean they saw each other away from work?"

"Yes, I believe so."

"Do you know of anybody else who might have been a friend of Miss Ortovsky?"

Miss Pynchon shook her head. "No, I don't know of anyone else. Laura might know, however."

"I'd like to see her."

"Surely," Miss Pynchon said. "Take a right at the end of this hall. Laura's office will be the fourth one on your left."

When Reardon entered her office Laura Murray was busily sketching designs on a pad of unlined paper. Her desk was covered with dress patterns, pencils and pieces of cloth. They seemed to flow over the desk like wax down the sides of a melting candle.

"Laura Murray?" Reardon asked.

She looked up quizzically. "That's me." She was dressed in a red turtleneck sweater, which in its brightness seemed less modest than the woman who wore it. She had a plain, undistinguished face—one, Reardon knew, that would be difficult to recall without a photograph.

Reardon pulled out his identification. "My name is John Reardon," he said. "I'm investigating the murders of Karen Ortovsky and her roommate."

He saw her face suddenly tense, but he did not know whether the change meant fear or embarrassment or sorrow. "I understand that you knew Miss Ortovsky. Socially, I mean. Away from work."

"Yes, I did." She nodded toward an empty chair. "Please sit down."

When Reardon had sat down Laura Murray stood up, quietly closed the door of her office, then returned to the chair behind her desk. She folded her hands in front of her and rested them on the desk. Reardon could see that they were trembling very slightly.

"How well did you know her?" he asked.

"We were close friends. We met here. She'd been working here for a year when I came. I guess I've known her for about four years."

Reardon noticed that when Laura Murray spoke to him she seemed to stare over his shoulder or down at some object on her desk, not wanting their eyes to meet. "There's no reason to be nervous, Miss Murray," he assured her. "This is just routine. Legwork, that's all. We have to interview everybody we can find who knew Miss Ortovsky."

She snapped a pencil from the top of her desk and rolled it between the fingertips of both her hands.

"So you knew her for about four years?" Reardon said.

"Yes. We were close friends."

Suddenly the door to the office opened. Laura started in her chair, and Reardon turned to see a short, middle-aged man standing in the doorway, his hand still resting on the doorknob. "Oh, sorry," he said. "I didn't know you were busy, Laura. Miss Pynchon just wants to know when your sketches will be ready."

"This afternoon," Laura snapped.

"Thanks," the man said. He retreated out of the doorway, carefully closing the door behind him.

Reardon could see that Laura was jittery, almost panicky. "Miss Murray," he said gently, "would you like to go for a walk with me? Someplace where we can talk privately?"

She smiled sadly. "Yes, that might be the best thing."

"There's a coffee shop just down the street," Reardon said. "It should be just about empty this time of day."

"Fine," Laura said.

At the coffee shop Reardon felt it necessary to make something very clear. "Miss Murray," he said, "we know a lot about Karen Ortovsky already. Or at least I think we do. What I mean is, we know . . ." Reardon stopped. He could not think of the right words. "We know her sexual habits." They were still not the right words, and Reardon knew it.

Laura looked at him with relief. "I see," she said. "I'm glad. There's no point in avoiding anything then. We had—Karen and I—we had the same—as you say —sexual habits."

"I'm only interested in this if it could have had anything to do with her death," Reardon said quickly. "Believe me, Miss Murray, it's of no importance to me. This is a murder investigation. I'm not concerned with anything else. I just want to know who killed Karen and her roommate."

"I didn't know her roommate very well," Laura said. "But before Lee came along Karen and I were very close. I don't know what you think about anything,

Mr. Reardon, but Karen was a good person, a sweet person."

"I'm sure she was," Reardon said, and he meant it. He suspected that the same could be said for Laura Murray.

"I loved her," she said. "For a while as a lover, then later as a friend. When I first came to New York from Virginia I didn't know anybody. I'm shy. It's hard for me to get to know people. For a year I didn't know anybody except the local grocer, people like that. People you just say 'hello' and 'good-bye' to, and that's it. Then I came to work at Tristan, and I met Karen. For a long time we were just friends. That's all. Just friends. We'd go to movies together, or to dinner, things like that. We even double-dated a few times. Then one night—after a double date, as a matter of fact—I stayed at her apartment. It was late and so rather than make my date go all the way to Brooklyn Heights with me on the subway, I just stayed with Karen. It seemed like the most reasonable thing to do." She stopped and looked at Reardon, evaluating him, then came to some decision in her mind. "We made love that night. I don't know how it happened. It just did."

The tension was gone from her face, and all the nervousness. She sat calmly, glancing occasionally out the window at nothing in particular. For a moment Reardon was lost in the spacious decency of her face. He wondered if that was what it felt like, to be released.

"When did you see her last?" he asked quietly.

"Wednesday. The Wednesday before she died. At work. I haven't seen Karen outside the office for two years. She met Lee, and after that I didn't see her anymore except at work."

"Did you know Lee?"

"Lee? I met her a few times when she would meet Karen at the office in the afternoon. That's all. But I know Karen must have been absolutely devoted to her. There was no other way for Karen. It had to be total or nothing."

"Did she have any other friends at the office?"

"No, not that I know of."

"Surely she must have been friendly with other people."

"They had mutual friends, I think. Karen and Lee, I mean. Sometimes they'd mention a name—a Phillip or a John or something like that—and it was obvious they both knew this person. So I guess they had friends, but I didn't know them."

"Do you know of any list of addresses or anything like that, something that Karen might have had somewhere other than her office or apartment? The police couldn't find anything."

"I know something about that," Laura said suddenly. "She didn't write addresses down. She said them over and over again until she had them memorized. A year after she started living with Lee I moved and changed my address. So I wanted Karen to know my new address. You know, in case she ever wanted to get in touch with me, needed help or something like that. But she wouldn't write it down."

"Did you ask her why?"

"Yeah, I said, 'Why don't you just write it down? Wouldn't that be easier?' "

"What did she say?"

"Now that you mention it, she looked a little strange when I asked her that, a little frightened or something, like she'd let down her guard or something like that. A little embarrassed maybe. She just said something about always memorizing these things. She said Lee thought it was a good idea. She said it trained her memory or something like that."

"She said Lee thought it was a good idea?"

"Yes," Laura said. "She definitely mentioned Lee."

11

After leaving Laura Murray Reardon went to the city morgue at Bellevue Hospital. He wanted to see the bodies of Lee McDonald and Karen Ortovsky once again and to see the pathologist's report.

He found Jake Simpson, a morgue attendant he'd known for years, reading a paperback novel at his desk. Years of menial labor at the command of other men vastly better educated and better paid had done a job on Simpson, grinding him down to a fine edge of resentment.

"What can I do for you?" Simpson asked glumly, putting his novel facedown on his desk. The crooked cigarette dangling from his mouth made him look like an aging pool hustler.

"I'd like to take a look at the report on the women in the Village, McDonald and Ortovsky."

Jake struggled to his feet. "I'll get them." He went to a gray metal file cabinet and extracted two manila envelopes from one of the drawers. "Here they are," he said. "Just came in."

"Thanks," Reardon said. He took the envelopes and pulled out a chair at an empty desk. "Okay if I sit here?"

"Who gives a shit," said Simpson, who had gone back to his paperback novel.

Reardon sat down and opened an envelope.

Jake peered up from the book. "She took a dump, you know."

Reardon looked over at him. "What are you talking about?"

"The one that got her throat cut," Jake said. "She took a terrible shit. Rothman said he'd never seen so much crap."

"Karen?"

"The one in the closet. Crapped her pants."

"She was scared out of her goddamn mind," Reardon said, feeling the heat of his anger rise in his face.

"Must of been," Jake said. He smiled. "Not that unusual, you know. Rothman's kind of new around here. Don't know his ass from a hole in the wall." He went back to his book.

Reardon turned to the first page of the pathologist's report on Lee McDonald. It was the usual, the same sterile language. Each of Lee's major organs had been cut out of her body and weighed in grams: heart, liver, pancreas, kidneys, everything. The lacerations received by each organ were recorded in centimeters. The contents of her stomach and intestines were recorded in cubic centimeters, with references to texture and color. The consistency of her feces was described as part fluid, part pulpy.

Reardon winced but continued reading. Even the arid language of the report suggested that her body had been cut to ribbons. But Mathesson had been right: Lee McDonald had not been sexually abused. There was no residue of semen in or around either the vagina or the anus.

Then he saw it. The definite connection. Lee Mc-

Donald had been stabbed fifty-seven times. These were direct, purposeful blows, deep and wide, not the numerous scratches and cuts any victim receives while fending off a blade with bare arms.

Quickly Reardon turned through the report on Karen Ortovsky. She had been stabbed only once.

The pathologist's report made the MO complete. Lee McDonald and Karen Ortovsky had been slaughtered exactly like the fallow deer.

Reardon walked back over to Jake's desk and handed him the report. "I'd like to see the bodies," he said.

"Didn't you see them down in the Village?" Jake asked.

"Yeah, but I want to check something."

"Sure you just don't have a taste for dead flesh?" Jake asked with a grin.

"Where are they?" Reardon said sharply.

Jake stood up. "Feeling kind of humorless today, huh? They caught one of them in Brooklyn, you know. Somebody in the morgue, I mean. Fucking a dead body."

"Where are they?" Reardon repeated.

Jake's face turned sour. "Follow me." He led Reardon into the morgue room and pointed down the corridor. "In there. Units 87 and 88. I'll be out at the desk if you need anything."

Reardon slowly made his way into the morgue room. It seemed unearthly, fastidiously clean, all scrubbed tile and stainless steel, not at all like a murder room. The bodies were kept in refrigerated vaults that hazily reflected the fluorescent lighting overhead. Unit 87 bore a single identification, a small printed label inserted in a square of aluminum on the door:

City of New York
Office of the Chief Medical Examiner

MORTUARY COMPARTMENT CARD

Compartment Number ... 87
Name ... Patricia Lee McDonald
Age ... 25   Color ... White
Date of Death ... 10/20/77
Received from ... New York City Police Dept
Date Received ... 11/20/77
Place of Death ... 12 W. 12th St.

Reardon placed his hand on the steel handle of the freezer, but he did not open it. He did not want to open it. In all his years on the force he had visited the morgue only once before. Visiting the dead here, in their cold, awesome vulnerability, had always seemed to him like an intolerable violation of that final right to dignity.

The one other time he had been here, five years ago, he had come to see the only human being he had ever put here. He had come late at night and been ushered into the same bright room with its antiseptic smell and garish lighting. His eyes had searched out a different number and a different name:

City of New York
Office of the Chief Medical Examiner

MORTUARY COMPARTMENT CARD

Compartment Number ... 93
Name ... Thomas Frederick Wilson
Age ... 29   Color ... White
Date of Death ... 7/22/72
Received from ... New York City Police Dept
Date received ... 7/22/72
Place of Death ... 274 E. 4th St.

When he had died at twenty-nine, Thomas Frederick Wilson had already assembled a long criminal record. He had turned relatively late to murder. But when he had, Reardon remembered, it was with abandon, killing five people in as many months. His plan had been to leave no witnesses to his robberies.

Wilson had had two problems, Reardon recalled. He had a big mouth and a buddy who liked to listen. In the end Wilson's friend had gone to the local precinct house and told Reardon everything.

That afternoon he and Mathesson had let themselves into Wilson's apartment and were in the midst of searching it when they heard footsteps on the stairs. Reardon retreated behind some of the clothes hanging in the closet and Mathesson ducked behind the sofa. Silently they listened as the sound of footsteps grew more distinct.

When the door opened and Wilson stepped into the apartment, Reardon saw that he was carrying a pistol in his right hand. For a moment Wilson did not move.

Then Mathesson shot up from behind the sofa. "Police!" he shouted. "Don't move!"

Over the barrel of his own gun Reardon saw Wilson level his pistol toward Mathesson and fire and Mathesson's body jerk to the left, tumbling across the edge of the bureau to the floor.

Then Reardon had fired. And for every day of the rest of his life he had recalled the thunderousness of his gun's report, which had seemed to deafen everything, plunging the world into a heavy, mourning silence. Wilson's chest had seemed to explode from below his skin, a bloom of crimson opening across his chest like the petals of a rose. He staggered backward, his face frozen in a look of childlike amazement, and it was the look on that face that had haunted Reardon forever afterward; he had never been able to describe it to anyone, not even to Millie, but he knew it would stay in his mind, like an unanswerable riddle, until the day he died.

It was the chill of the handle on his fingers that brought Reardon's mind back now. He looked at the nameplate on the door. Patricia Lee McDonald. He released the handle and slid his hand deep into the pocket of his overcoat. Patricia Lee McDonald had been violated enough for one life, he thought, and the fallow deer too, and all the others. He turned and left the morgue.

12

WEEKEND

On Saturday morning Mathesson telephoned Reardon to tell him he had not been able to dig anything up on Lee McDonald. Mathesson said that on Friday he had gone to the law firm where she had worked for the last five years, but that no one knew very much about her. She had no friends at the firm and did not seem to have confided anything about her private life to anyone.

"I talked to just about everybody in the office," Mathesson said, "except for some high rollers off on a junket to Las Vegas."

"And you got nothing at all?"

"Nothing."

"All right," Reardon said. "See you Monday."

There was still another possibility and late in the weekend Reardon tried it.

On Sunday afternoon funeral services for Patricia Lee McDonald were held at Saint Jude's Catholic Church in Brooklyn. Reardon went. He sat in the back of the church, his hat resting on his lap, his overcoat neatly folded beside him, and listened to the drone of the Mass, the old beseechments for the forgiveness of Lee McDonald's sins and the salvation of her soul. At the front of the church he could see the coffin, closed, unadorned by flowers, resting before the altar.

For a moment he imagined the body inside, chill, pallid, bloodless, the pathologist's incisions sewed up with thick black thread.

Besides Reardon and the priest, there were only three other people in the church. Reardon remembered his father's funeral. It had been a crowded affair, cops and their families squeezing together in the pews, and the people from the neighborhood decked out in their Sunday best. His mother had told him at the time it was the kind of funeral that happened only "when a good man dies."

This funeral was different. When the services were over, Reardon made his way to the front of the church. An older couple he assumed to be Lee McDonald's parents were getting into a car behind the hearse. A younger man stood silently beside a red Volkswagen, waiting for the hearse to leave for the cemetery.

Reardon stood on the church steps beside the priest until the funeral procession had pulled away. Then he took out his gold shield and wordlessly displayed it to the priest.

The priest looked at him. "I see," he said quietly.

"I wonder if I might have a moment of your time, Father?"

"I have to be on my way to the cemetery shortly," the priest said.

"I know," Reardon said. "It won't take long."

"Go ahead then." The priest put out his hand. "I'm Father Perry." He was an old man, but the skin of his face was still tightly drawn across high cheekbones. He had once been a handsome man, Reardon surmised, which, in itself, must have been an almost irresistible occasion for sin. His hair was close-cropped and very white, which gave him the appearance of a retired military officer. He stood erect, but Reardon could detect a certain weakness in his legs, as if they were aging more rapidly than the body they supported.

"Did you know Miss McDonald very well?" Reardon asked. It felt incongruous, this litany of investigation on the steps of a church. On the sunny Brooklyn street cars went past. A boy walked past bouncing a rubber ball.

"I knew Patty all her life," Father Perry said. "I baptized her."

"You called her Patty?"

"Everyone did. I understand from her father that later on she started going by her other name. Lee."

"Why was that?" Reardon asked.

Father Perry cleared his throat. He seemed to be trying to calculate what was proper for him to say and what to hold back. "Well, you see," he said finally, "Patty had a lot of trouble in her life."

"What kind of trouble?"

"Family trouble," Father Perry admitted gently. He looked about hesitantly, as if assuring himself that he and Reardon were not being overheard. "Mostly what I see is the sin of gossip," he said. "You hear so much sometimes that you come to think the walls must be giving up their secrets."

"What kind of trouble was she having with her parents?" Reardon asked.

"Well, she wanted to go one way. They wanted her to go another way. That sort of thing."

"What way?"

"Well, to tell you the truth, they wanted her to be just like them. It's very common." He spoke gently, kindly, like a man who had seen a great deal of distress in his life, none of it very original.

Reardon adopted Father Perry's language. "What way did they want her to go?"

"They wanted her to be a family person." Father Perry smiled faintly. "Blooming with child every ten months, inviting them over for the Saint Patrick's Day feast or Christmas dinner, living like they lived, wanting what they wanted."

Reardon nodded. "And what way did she want for herself?"

"She wanted to get out of Brooklyn for one thing," Father Perry said. He glanced dully at the long line of row houses on the opposite side of the street and the endless stretch of late-model cars parked in front of them. "She always hated Brooklyn. Even as a child. You should have seen the disgust in her face. I remember telling her once—almost as a joke, you understand—that it's the sin of vanity to hate a place so much."

"She thought she had better things to do?"

"Oh, yes, positively," Father Perry said. "I think she had—what is it they call them these days?—" He smiled ironically, indulgently—"artistic drives."

Reardon nodded.

"She paid a terrible price, Mr. Reardon," Father Perry added.

"Yes, she did."

"But she couldn't have stayed here in Brooklyn. She'd have gone insane. She was like a tiger in a zoo, that one. And she thought Brooklyn was her cage, but she probably thought her family was the worst cage of all." Father Perry looked out in the direction of Manhattan. "It reminds me of a story, you know. I can't remember where I heard it. But it seems there was a woman who complained to her priest that in the place where she lived her father had been eaten by tigers, and her mother, and her husband and all her children. All of them, eaten by tigers. So naturally the priest asked the woman why she kept living in such a terrible place. And she said that at least in that place there was no oppression." Father Perry smiled benignly. "For Patty anything was better than living with her family in Brooklyn." He nodded toward Manhattan. "Even out there, among the tigers."

"When did she leave Brooklyn?" Reardon asked.

"When she was twenty, I think."

"Where did she go?"

"Where else? Manhattan. That's the Lourdes of the artistically driven, I hear."

"And that upset her family? Her moving to Manhattan, I mean?"

"It more than upset them," Father Perry said. "But I think there was more to it than that. I'm just an old priest, not God. I don't know everything. But I think there was something else. Anyway, they disowned her. Told her she was dead as far as they were concerned." He rubbed his eyes sleepily. "It's been a long day," he said.

"Yeah," Reardon said.

Father Perry glanced at his watch. "I'm sorry," he said, "but I have to be on my way. They'll be at the cemetery soon, and nobody appreciates having these things drawn out."

"I understand," Reardon said. "Thank you, Father."

"Anyway," Father Perry said, "there's somebody else who could tell you more about Patty than I could. I just hear things from her parents, and they don't know much, to tell you the truth. Patty pretty much wrote them off. However, you might try her husband, Jamie O'Rourke."

"Her husband?"

"Used to be," Father Perry said. "As far as the

Church is concerned they're still married. You didn't know she was married, that she had a husband?"

"No," Reardon said. "Where is he?"

"You just missed him. He was at the funeral. The only one here besides Patty's parents. Tall young man. You must have seen him. He left for the cemetery in that little red car of his."

"Yes, I know who you mean," Reardon said. "Where does he live?"

"Not far from here," Father Perry said. He gave Reardon the address and Reardon carefully wrote it down in his notebook.

"Thank you for your trouble, Father."

"It's like they say," Father Perry replied, "trouble is my business."

He turned away from Reardon and began to descend the worn stone steps. He moved unsteadily, tightly gripping the banister, slowly lowering himself from one step to another, like an old shepherd moving reluctantly, dutifully, toward his leaden-eyed and inconsolable flock.

13

That night Reardon did not go to bed until almost
dawn. Instead he watched television, or at least he
stared at the television set. Watching the next program,
he could not have described the previous one. The
dramas and comedies passed one after the other without for a single moment deflecting Reardon's mind
from the killing of the fallow deer.

Again he went over the details of the case. Two
dead deer. Two dead women. Fifty-seven blows on one
body and only one massive blow on the other. The
word "dos" and Roman numeral "two." A witness
who saw the girls with a third party shortly before
they were killed but could not identify the third party.
Lesbianism. A sound in the zoo at about the time the
deer were being killed, a sound simultaneously muffled
and harsh. No weapon. No witnesses to the crime itself. And Andros Petrakis.

Reardon went over each of the people associated
with the case so far. And each time only Andros
Petrakis stood out. He had reason to hate Wallace Van
Allen, whose associates had evicted him from his apartment. He had openly expressed hatred of his landlord.
He had been present near the scene of the crime shortly
before it was committed. And there was at least a
chance that he had already lied through his daughter.
In addition to these tangible connections there was

131

added the fact that he had been under an enormous strain in the past few weeks. The death of his wife had stunned him, and her illness had impoverished him. Cases, Reardon knew, had been built on less material than he had on Andros Petrakis. There was, for example, the case of Kevin Martin Dowd.

The body of twelve-year-old Kevin Dowd had been found in an alley off East 101st Street on a rainy Saturday morning in 1963, the face mutilated almost beyond recognition, the ears actually severed from the head and evidently taken by the killer. There were no clues, and it had struck Reardon at the time that this kind of crime, if not repeated, might easily go unsolved forever.

Then it happened. The odd, unexplainable circumstance which cried out for explanation. Reardon, while routinely going through the personal effects of Kevin Dowd, discovered a school paper, a short book report not unlike thousands of others that public school teachers assigned their students during a school year. On the back of the paper the teacher had assigned the grade "F," and had written in huge letters across the face of the front page: "STUPID! STUPID! STUPID!" And Reardon had been driven to learn what kind of person would scrawl such an angry and humiliating comment on the insignificant book report of a twelve-year-old boy.

An investigation showed that the teacher, Randolph Devereaux, had repeatedly attacked Kevin Dowd in class, often reducing him to tears. On one occasion Devereaux had forced the boy to stand at the front of the room with his arms outstretched, holding two heavy books in each hand. This had lasted for several minutes until the boy's arms had collapsed from the strain.

Two weeks later Reardon went to Devereaux's apartment and introduced himself as a detective from the New York City Police Department. Reardon would always remember how Devereaux's body had suddenly slumped, every feature of his face sinking downward, and how he had sounded almost relieved when he'd said, "You must be looking for the ears."

A one-in-a-million chance, thought Reardon, just like Gustave Lamprey.

Whatever fame Reardon had in the New York City Police Department rested in part on the Lamprey case.

While still a uniformed patrolman Reardon had been called to a disturbance in a movie theater in Chinatown. A young man had made a nuisance of himself by continually shouting obscenities at the characters on the screen. Several people in the theater had unsuccessfully attempted to quiet him. Finally an usher was called and when he told Lamprey that he would either have to keep quiet or leave the theater, Lamprey pulled a machete. "I don't speak Chinese," he said to the usher, even though the usher had addressed him in English.

The usher quickly apologized for disturbing Lamprey, excused himself, and walked briskly back to the lobby of the theater and called the police.

Reardon and another patrolman, Harry Flynn, arrived at the theater lobby ten minutes later. The usher escorted them down the aisle and pointed to the back of Lamprey's head. Reardon told Flynn to cover him from behind and cautiously descended the aisle toward Lamprey. As if warned by some private guardian, Lamprey shot out of his seat just as Reardon reached the row where he was sitting. He turned and faced Reardon, not more than four feet away.

Lamprey was very tall, thin and straight as an ice-

pick, with bright, searching eyes. But the thing that
Reardon would remember most was that he wore
an unusual metal ring shaped into a dragon's head. The
eyes of the dragon were enormous, grotesquely dispro-
portionate with the head, and they were made of deep
red glass, the deepest red that Reardon had ever seen.
The hand wearing the ring carried a wicked-looking
machete.

"Mister," Reardon said, "there's another policeman
behind you and he's pointing a pistol right at your
head."

"I don't speak Chinese," Lamprey said.

"I'm talking to you in English," Reardon said. "Now
I want you to put your hands behind your head and
move very slowly toward me and into this aisle."

Lamprey cocked his head as if receiving instructions
from some invisible force. Then he smiled at Reardon
and complied.

Gustave Lamprey was booked for disorderly conduct
and possession of a concealed weapon, and Reardon
did not expect to ever hear of him again. But almost
twenty years later he did.

It was in the summer and he was examining a corpse
found on a tenement roof. The body had been deposited
on the roof and left there to bake in the hot July sun.
It was bloated, blackened, nude except for a pair of
socks. It lay on its back, legs together, arms stretched
perpendicular to the trunk like the spread wings of a
fallen bird. There was nothing unusual except for tiny
bits of red glass which had been ground almost to a
powder and sprinkled ceremoniously over the dead
man's chest. It was the color of the glass which drew
Reardon's attention. It was not just red, but deep red,
and Reardon could not recall where he had seen that
color before, if he ever had. He stared at the body for

a while, knowing that something was familiar about it, but he could not tell what.

He walked down the stairs to the street, and as he neared the entrance of the building he glanced at the nameplates on the mailboxes. One of them brought the colored glass into rigid focus in his mind. It was printed neatly in black type: "Institute for Chinese Studies—Gustave Lamprey, Director."

And it was that chance connection—the vague familiarity of the deep red color of glass, and the sudden memory from twenty years before of the minor arrest of a man with an odd name and an obsession with things Chinese—that had led Reardon to a chain of evidence and an airtight case that had made him famous among his peers.

A one-in-a-million chance, Reardon thought again. He did not believe that any sudden revelations would come forth to solve the case of the fallow deer. It was, he knew, the more mundane details that broke a case, or incriminating evidence left at the scene, or obvious motive, or, better yet, eyewitnesses. In the deer case there was none of these. There was only the crime itself, its brutal details, and a floating cryptogram of numbers: fifty-seven, one, two.

14

MONDAY

When he arrived at the precinct house on Monday morning Reardon was informed that the weapon thought to have been used in the killing of the fallow deer had been discovered. It was Piccolini who told him, a delighted smile decorating his face. Even his office seemed to have taken on an airiness Reardon had never noticed.

"Who found it?" Reardon asked.

"Trash detail."

"Where'd they find it?"

"In a sewer under Fifth Avenue."

"Fifth Avenue?" Reardon was surprised. "I expected the killer to head out through the park, not on to Fifth Avenue."

"Yeah," Piccolini said, "me too. But maybe we're dealing with a guy who's not too sophisticated. A nut." Piccolini smiled. "I think we've got him. If he was crazy enough to run up on Fifth Avenue, then he's crazy enough to have left his fingerprints. The lab's checking for 'em now."

"What was the weapon?" Readon asked.

"A double-edged ax. But there's more than that. It was a Parks Department ax. Had 'Property of New York City' written on it!"

Petrakis, Reardon thought. "I'm going to put out an all-points bulletin on Andros Petrakis," he said.

"He shouldn't be hard to find," Piccolini said. "A person at loose ends like that, crazy and all, he'll leave a trail a blind man could follow. We'll have him in custody by the end of the week."

"Unless the ax points to someone else."

"Not likely. He hated Van Allen and so he took a Parks Department ax and killed those deer to get even." Piccolini smiled. "He should have known that nobody gets even with a guy like Wallace Van Allen. Nobody. No way."

"Have the Van Allens been told about the ax?" Reardon asked.

"For sure. They get a daily report on the case."

"Well, hold back a few details for Christ's sake," Reardon said irritably. "I mean, this is a criminal investigation. You need to hold back some details."

Piccolini looked up. "Look, I know what I'm doing in this case. And we're going to break this case. And it's going to stick. Personally, I think we've got our man, and that's all there is to it. This thing will be wrapped up by the end of the week."

"What about the women?" Reardon asked.

Piccolini looked at Reardon quizzically. "What women?"

"The women in the Village."

"Oh," Piccolini said, "those women. Well, I don't know. Probably no connection there."

"I think there is," Reardon said, convincing himself of it.

Piccolini looked at Reardon scornfully. "You know, you're really somethin', John. At first you didn't think there was a connection. No reason, you just didn't think so. Now you think there is. Do you have a reason?"

"Only what you know."

"Only the same number of wounds on the bodies of the deer and the women, right?"

"That's right," Reardon admitted. "And the numbers."

"Forget about the numbers. That doesn't mean anything. And you know as well as I do that pathologists have a hard time determining exactly how many wounds are deliberately inflicted on a victim. They come up with a guess, really. And by coincidence they came up with the same guesses for the deer and the women in the Village. To tell you the truth, I don't think it means a thing. So drop the connection between the cases."

Reardon glared at Piccolini.

"I mean it," Piccolini said. "Drop it! You just keep yourself busy finding that little Greek guy. It's ridiculous that he hasn't been located yet. Ridiculous! And I want him! Fast!"

Reardon turned to leave.

"And, John," Picolini said, "maybe you didn't take a long enough vacation."

"I'll tell you when I need a vacation," Reardon snapped.

"Think about it," Piccolini said, "think about it real good. My reading of the situation downtown tells me that they're not too happy with the way you're handling this case."

"Then let them tell me," Reardon said.

"Just think about it," Piccolini said, "think about it real good."

Reardon did not know why he thought there was a connection between the killing of the fallow deer and the murders of Karen Ortovsky and Lee McDonald. Piccolini had been right when he pointed out the inexactitude of the pathologist's report. There was also a problem in determining how many wounds were direct thrusts on the part of the assailant and how many were defensive wounds caused by the victim's attempts to protect herself from the attacker.

Reardon decided to check out the most obvious connection first; later that afternoon he called the Department of Buildings and confirmed that the building in which the two women had lived, like Petrakis' building, was owned by Wallace Van Allen.

"Do you think that makes a connection?" Reardon asked Mathesson. They were at Reardon's desk, Mathesson leaning against it, a cup of coffee in his hand.

"Not an important one," Mathesson said. "Wallace Van Allen owns half the city. It could be a coincidence, but maybe not. Maybe Petrakis didn't get enough revenge by killing the deer. Maybe he went after human victims. But I get the feeling you're not going after Petrakis."

"What do you mean?" Reardon asked.

Mathesson looked as if he did not want to answer. He took a quick sip from the coffee cup. "I get the feeling that you're after somebody else," he said. "Some other killer. Maybe Wallace Van Allen himself."

"I would never do that," Reardon said.

"Well, don't you think Petrakis did it, killed those deer?"

"He may have. But he may have killed Karen Ortovsky and Lee McDonald too."

"Why?"

"For the same reason you said. Maybe he's completely crazy. Maybe he intends to kill someone in every building Van Allen owns."

"You don't think he's crazy enough to believe he can bring down Van Allen's empire by scaring everybody who lives in one of his buildings, do you?"

"If he's insane, he could believe anything," Reardon said.

"Van Allen would hire an army before he'd let that happen."

"Of course he would," Reardon said, "and any sane person would know that. But what if this Petrakis *is* insane? Couldn't he have an idea like that? And do we have to wait till somebody else gets chopped up in one of Van Allen's buildings to do something about it?"

Mathesson laughed and draped his arm affectionately around Reardon's shoulders. "I don't know, John," he said. "I don't know about you and your theories."

For a long time Reardon sat at his desk going over the investigation to see if Mathesson could be right, if he really had been aiming the investigation away from Petrakis. It was true that, having met him, he did not like Wallace Van Allen very much. But Van Allen's condescension toward him was not noticeably different from that which he had experienced from others like Van Allen in the past. Perhaps he did have an added measure of hostility toward Van Allen because the man had been able to pull him off homicide and put him on the deer case. Still, he did not believe he was "after" Van Allen. In thirty years on the force he had never been "after" anyone.

He was still weighing the evidence against himself when the phone rang.

"John Reardon," he said.

"John, this is Josh down at the lab. I've got the findings on the ax. The one in the deer case."

"Go ahead."

"Well, there are prints."

"Whose?"

"Only one set. Traced them to an Andros Pe . . . Pee . . ."

"Petrakis?"

"Yeah, that's it. Petrakis. Somebody didn't write it down very well on the sheet."

"Andros Petrakis," Reardon said. "You're sure?"

"That's right. And only one set."

"Thanks," Reardon said, and started to hang up.

"There's one detail," Josh said. "Damndest thing, I don't know if it's important, but the positioning of the prints is kind of unusual."

"What do you mean?"

"Well, this was an ax killing, right?" Josh said.

"Right."

"Well, where would you expect the prints to be located?"

"On the handle."

"Right. But the weapon is clean for about two-thirds of the length of the ax handle."

"What?"

"From the bottom of the handle."

"Can you give me that again?"

"Ah, hell, if you were here it would be clear in a minute. The ax handle is approximately three feet long from the bottom of the handle to the blade. And from the bottom of the handle to about eight inches from the blade the handle is clean. No prints. But after that, the damn thing is covered with prints. Of this Petrakis guy. His prints. Clear as day. Hell, you could almost see them without dusting."

"I see," Reardon said, but he did not know what to make of it.

"The prints begin at about four inches below the blade. And there are a few on the blade itself."

Reardon was mystified. "Do you know what this means? Do you have any ideas?"

"Nothing for sure. The only thing I can figure out is that maybe he had started to clean up the prints, and then he got scared or something and just took off. Decided to hide the thing and just forget about it, you know?"

"Thanks, Josh," Reardon said, and placed the receiver back on the cradle. So Petrakis had started to clean it up, he thought, but then had left it there with prints still on it. Maybe he had heard something. Maybe he had heard the same thing Noble had heard. Maybe he had heard the only thing that would make him run, make him panic so much that he would just leave his prints on the ax and hope that it wouldn't be found. Maybe he had heard the approach of a witness.

Looking at the ax later that afternoon, Reardon got a better idea of what Josh had told him. While Mathesson stood with his hands behind his back, his eyes roaming the lab for something more interesting than a routine weapon, Reardon stared fixedly at the ax. It lay on its side atop a metal table. Most of the handle had indeed been cleaned meticulously of fingerprints. Reardon had rarely seen a weapon so thoroughly scrubbed in part and so completely untouched elsewhere. Killers who used knives, Reardon had noticed, usually did not stop after cleaning the handle but dutifully wiped the blood from the blade as well, even though it could not possibly incriminate them. They did this from habit, Reardon assumed, but the ax used in the killing of the fallow deer presented a paradox that could neither be explained nor altogether dismissed.

He picked up the ax and perused the handle slowly. It was spotless from the base up to about seven or eight inches from the blade. Then spots of blood began to dapple the wood. The blade itself was almost completely sheathed in bloodstains.

Mathesson motioned toward the ax. "Well, that's it," he said. "When you've got the weapon, you've got the killer."

"Not always."

"Sometimes," Mathesson said. He pulled out a pack of cigarettes and offered one to Reardon.

"No, thanks," Reardon said.

"Oh, right," Mathesson said. "I forgot. You quit."

Reardon's eyes remained riveted on the ax. In the presence of a weapon he became almost reverent, not out of respect for the weapon itself but for the human being, obscure and silent, who had been slaughtered by it.

"Do you watch much TV?" Mathesson asked.

"What?"

"Do you watch much TV?"

"A little."

"They had a goddamn good show on last night." Mathesson chuckled. "A real whodunit, you know? First I thought it was the wife, then the lover, then the brother-in-law. Hell, I'd have put the whole goddamn family in the slammer before I'd have fingered the right guy."

Reardon's eyes continued to move up and down the ax. Mathesson's voice was recorded only as passing unintelligible sounds, like street noise.

Finally, Reardon said: "What do you make of that?"

"What?"

"The way the ax is so thoroughly cleaned of prints on part of the handle and covered with them on the rest."

Mathesson looked at the ax. "Well, the only thing I figure is that the killer got scared, panicked, started running, and threw the ax in the sewer drain on Fifth Avenue. And if the killer is Petrakis, then it stands to reason he might run east up to Fifth Avenue, 'cause he lives on the East Side, East Ninetieth, right?"

"That's his old address, but remember, he'd been evicted. We don't know where he was living the night the deer were killed."

"Oh, yeah," Mathesson said, "that's right." He looked at the ax again. "I'll admit that a guy who'd clean a weapon as good as this guy did, you could expect him to clean the whole thing, not leave any prints. But who knows what was going through his mind? And remember, John, those prints belong to Petrakis and nobody else. Now, I figure he just plain bolted. Just plain panicked. Forgot everything. Just started running home."

"If his new address is on the East Side."

"Right," Mathesson said. "And another thing. That ax came from a toolshed not far from the deer cage. I just got this from Bannion this morning. I asked Bannion to check and see if it looked like the toolshed had been broken into, and he said no. He said that whoever took that ax had to have had a key to the shed."

"Who has access to the shed?"

"Noble, Bryant and Petrakis. The regular night crew. I talked to Bryant just before I came over, and Bannion talked to Noble last night. They hadn't been using the ax. Noble said he saw it in the shed earlier that night when he went to take out something else."

"So it had to have been in there," Reardon said, "and whoever took it out had to have had a key."

"That's right," Mathesson said. "Everything's right for Petrakis."

"All right," Reardon said, "what's your idea of the whole thing, from beginning to end?"

"Well," Mathesson said, "I figure Petrakis was real upset. His wife dying and all, you know. And on top of his wife dying and this costing him all his money, he gets kicked out of his apartment. So that sets him off, you know? Puts him over the brink, you might say. He's real agitated by now. Crazy. So he goes to the park, maybe just to walk around at first, who knows? Anyway, he goes to the zoo and on the way he meets Bryant. He's so mad that the only thing he can talk about is his lousy landlord. Which is none other than your friend and mine, Wallace Van Allen."

"You think he'd have known who his landlord was?" Reardon asked.

"I don't know, to be honest with you. Of course, that stuff is in the public record. Anybody has access to it. Anybody can find out who their landlord is."

"But it takes a while to track it down."

"Yeah," Mathesson said, "but look at it this way: I once had a buddy who lived in a building on East 72nd Street. Now, normally he wouldn't know who his landlord was. Just some corporation, you know what I mean? But it so happened that his building was owned by some movie star—I forget who it was exactly—but a big Hollywood star, you know? So my buddy knew who owned the building. Kind of took pride in it, you know? Like it made him kind of different, kind of important or special or something, living in a building owned by a famous person."

"Yeah," Reardon said.

"Well, Wallace Van Allen is a big name, you know what I mean? So Petrakis could have known who his landlord was without going through the hassle of researching it. I'd be willing to bet that if you canvassed Petrakis' old building the tenants would know that Wallace Van Allen owned the building they live in."

This made sense to Reardon. He leaned on the metal table and concentrated his attention on Mathesson. "Go on."

"Well," Mathesson said, "Petrakis goes to the zoo. Now remember, he's goofy. He takes the ax and decides to get even with Van Allen. So he kills the deer in a crazy rage. Uncontrollable, you might say."

"Why did he kill them like he did?"

"What do you mean?"

"Why did he cut one of them to ribbons with fifty-seven different wounds and then kill the other one with a single blow?"

"Maybe he was tired," Mathesson said. "What he did to that first deer would take a lot out of you. In any case, after he's through with the killing, he starts cleaning the fingerprints off the ax. He probably plans to put the ax back in the toolshed. Then he hears something, maybe that muffled and grating sound Noble heard. Anyway, he panics. He forgets about cleaning the goddamn ax and just decides to ditch it."

"On Fifth Avenue?"

"That's right," Mathesson said, visibly warming to the narrative. "But he sees he's on a city street that could have witnesses, and there he is holding a goddamn ax that's dripping with blood, so he pitches it in the sewer drain under the street. And that's it. He takes off for home." Mathesson took a deep breath and exhaled slowly, clearly pleased with his account.

For a moment there was silence, while Reardon

thought about the scenario just presented by Mathesson. "So Petrakis took off toward home?" he asked finally. "Remember, we don't know where he lives since he was evicted."

"The chances are he stayed on the East Side. I'll bet when you find his new address, it'll be on the East Side."

"It may be," Reardon admitted.

"May be, bullshit!" Mathesson laughed, shrugging off the frustration that Reardon could see building in him. "Well," he said, "we may have the clincher anyway."

"What clincher?"

"It may not be sure," Mathesson said with a teasing smile, "but it's a chance. That kid, Daniels."

"The kid with the cocaine bust?"

"That's right. I finally got through to him."

"So?"

"I got through that goddamn wall of legal eagles his rich papa hired to get the little prick off the hook," Mathesson said proudly. "He's coming in to talk to us. He may have seen something."

Daniels might have the answer, Reardon thought. Cases had been broken that way before, and Reardon hoped the killing of the fallow deer and of the women in the Village could be solved quickly. He was not sure why this case disturbed him so particularly. He only knew that it did, and he wanted to escape the pressures he could feel building in himself with every hour it remained unsolved. "When's he coming in?" he asked.

"He should be here in an hour or so. Piccolini offered to have the questioning done at the kid's place, but the kid's father said that he'd rather it all be done down here." Mathesson grinned. "He probably thought we'd come roaring up with our sirens blasting, and that wouldn't look too good on Fifth Avenue."

Reardon pulled out the arrest sheet for the morning the fallow deer were killed and looked at it. "Winthrop Lewis Daniels," he said.

"His father must be scared shitless." Mathesson popped a piece of hard candy into his mouth and started moving it from one side of his mouth to the other. "The old man probably figures we're gonna try to pin a heavy rap on his darling boy."

"Heavier than possession of cocaine?"

Mathesson flicked his hand in a gesture of dismissal. "Ah, they won't even pin that on him. This will be strictly a probation rap. You don't stick a possession charge on an Upper East Side kid. You know what I mean. This is strictly a bad bust, a lot of paperwork for nothing." Mathesson winked at Reardon. "Like the Spics say in the Barrio, 'Nada, nada and more nada.'"

Reardon nodded. It had always been this way, he thought. But it was becoming more difficult for him to accept it.

Mathesson started buttoning his overcoat. "Well," he said, "have a jolly time of it. I got to be in court this morning. I got to testify against this nigger whore." He smiled. "She wasted her pimp—stuck a blade in his guts and pulled up on it." He thrust an imaginary blade in his abdomen and jerked upward. "Hari kari pickaninny style." He shook his head in disgust. "Hell, I don't know why they bother to charge her. Son of a bitch got what he deserved. He was a white dude, too —honky, ofay, you know what I mean? Probably a lot of goddamn feeling went into that blade, you know what I mean? Getting even in spades you might say."

Mathesson shook with laughter and slapped his leg. "Goddamn, I'm in a good mood," he said.

Reardon could not imagine why.

Mathesson told him. "I believe we busted this case. I believe we got that Petrakis cold."

"Yeah," Reardon said weakly.

Mathesson straightened his tie and stood erect. "Well," he said, "do I look—what do the lawyers call it?—credible?"

Reardon nodded.

"Well, take it easy." Mathesson started toward the door. "I'll see you this afternoon."

"Right," Reardon said. Or wrong, he thought, dead wrong.

15

When Reardon returned to his desk, he stared down at the night update for the day the fallow deer were killed. It was full of names that ended in "a" and "o" and "ski," along with a number of names that were familiar enough; in most cases, Reardon knew, these were black names, old slave names like Johnson or Phillips. Beside these, the clean contours of the name Winthrop Lewis Daniels stood out like a silver spoon in a dung heap. Winthrop Lewis Daniels was the kind of name that had a stiff upper lip, knew its whereabouts at all times, and moved about with its own predetermined and resolute self-confidence. It was the kind of name that had an opinion on every issue and expected to be heard whenever it wished. It was not the kind of name that waited bleeding in the chaotic emergency receiving room of Bellevue Hospital or held close affection for a mongrel dog.

When Winthrop Lewis Daniels finally arrived at the precinct house, he was not alone. Reardon recognized him instantly even though he had never seen him before. Daniels was flanked on either side by two well-dressed men, each holding tightly to a briefcase. Not many teenage offenders came through the precinct house doors like that. From his desk Reardon watched as the three men approached the desk sergeant, who responded to one of their questions by pointing to Reardon.

"Detective Reardon?" one of the men asked as they approached his desk.

"That's right."

"My name is Colin Tower." He was a very tall, very thin man with coal black hair slicked down flat across his head. He did not offer his hand.

The bald, stocky man on his left Mr. Tower introduced as Mr. Arington. "We are here to represent Mr. Daniels in this matter," Mr. Tower said. He nodded toward the tall, thin young man to his right.

"Have a seat," Reardon said. He did not expect this to be easy. He had dealt with lawyers of the Tower-Arington variety before. It would be part of their strategy to frustrate him as much as possible. Once they had taken seats across from his desk, however, they looked somewhat less formidable.

Before Reardon could ask his first question, Mr. Tower spoke again. "Let me begin by saying that Mr. Daniels is quite willing to cooperate with the police. He has come of his own free will and any statement which he wishes to make will be regarded as completely voluntary."

Reardon nodded indifferently. He had heard it all before.

"If at any time Mr. Daniels wishes to conclude this interview," Mr. Tower went on, "we will have to insist that it be immediately terminated. We also reserve the right to advise Mr. Daniels of those questions upon which we feel he would be better served to remain wholly silent."

"I understand that you represent Mr. Daniels," Reardon said brusquely. "As far as I'm concerned Mr. Daniels is here voluntarily. But this is a serious investigation, and I think he would be well advised to cooperate with us."

"Pardon me," Mr. Arington said, "but we will decide the extent of Mr. Daniels' cooperation."

"That's fine," Reardon replied dryly.

Reardon looked at Mr. Tower. "According to an arrest sheet for last Monday in this precinct, Mr. Daniels was arrested for possession of cocaine."

Mr. Tower chuckled. "Absurd charge."

"I'm not trying the case," Reardon said.

"Of course not," said Mr. Tower. "It's just that the charge is so ludicrous."

"Absolutely no evidence," Mr. Arington said.

"I don't care about that," Reardon said. "But the fact is that he *was* arrested."

"He was arrested," Mr. Tower muttered reluctantly. He glanced knowingly at Mr. Arington, then back to Reardon.

Reardon pulled a map of Central Park from his desk drawer and unfolded it on top of his desk.

"What is this all about?" Mr. Tower asked. "We're perfectly aware of where Mr. Daniels was arrested. We don't require a map."

"I'm not investigating a cocaine bust," Reardon said. "That's not what I'm doing here."

"Then what are you doing?" Mr. Tower said. "Have you lost your mind? Do you have any idea of the kind of lawsuit you're going to be facing if you persist in your harassment of this young man?"

"I haven't harassed anybody," Reardon declared. "I'm trying to investigate two murders."

Mr. Tower popped to his feet. "Murders?"

Reardon looked at Mr. Tower wearily. "I told you that this is an investigation. Nobody is accusing Mr. Daniels of anything."

"What kind of murders?" Daniels asked quietly.

Mr. Tower leveled a cold stare at Daniels. "Don't

bother yourself about it. We'll handle this." He looked at Reardon. "This is outrageous. We understood from Mr. Piccolini that some police matter would be discussed this morning. We assumed that it would pertain to the utterly false charge already made against Mr. Daniels. But we had no idea that any attempt would be made to associate him with homicides."

"Are they homicides?" Daniels asked quietly.

"Winthrop, please," Mr. Arington pleaded. "You must let us handle this."

Reardon spoke directly, and quietly, to Daniels. "There's more than the homicides. We're not sure if they are connected with the rest."

"That's quite enough," Mr. Tower exclaimed.

Daniels looked thoughtfully at Reardon but said nothing.

"What do you think, Mr. Daniels?" Reardon asked, trying to strike through the wall of lawyers that separated them. Daniels did not appear at all like the spoiled child Langhof had described. He looked confused and a little worried. But more importantly, Reardon sensed that Daniels *did* know something and wanted to tell him about it.

Daniels stared quietly at Reardon.

"You saw something, didn't you?" Reardon asked.

"That's enough!" Mr. Tower exclaimed.

Daniels did not seem to hear Mr. Tower. He continued to stare at Reardon's face, and for a moment Reardon saw him not as a pampered delinquent, but as a pained young man, barely out of childhood, confronting something dreadful, confronting it fully, for perhaps the first time.

"What was it you saw?" Reardon asked firmly.

Mr. Tower grasped Daniels' arm. "I think we'd better go, Winthrop."

Daniels jerked his arm from Mr. Tower's grasp. "Sit down," he told him.

"Winthrop, stop it!" Tower said. He remained standing but did not resume his grasp of Daniels' arm.

Daniels looked at Reardon as if trying to determine something about his character, whether he could be trusted. "Was it in the park?"

"Yes," Reardon replied. "Two deer were killed."

"Deer?" Daniels asked with surprise. "Am I a suspect?"

Reardon nodded cautiously. "You might be."

"You see?" Mr. Tower warned. "You're a possible suspect."

Reardon continued. "The deer were killed in the Children's Zoo. You were near the deer cage only a few minutes after they were killed."

Mr. Tower looked at Reardon, then at Daniels. "Winthrop, please don't get yourself any deeper in this. You don't know how the police operate."

Daniels continued to look straight into Reardon's eyes. "I didn't have anything to do with killing those deer," he said calmly. "But I may know who did."

Mr. Tower slumped down in his chair. "That's it," he said. "At this point, Winthrop, I would advise you to tell Mr. Reardon everything you know about this case."

"Thank you, Mr. Tower," Reardon said politely. He looked at Daniels. "What do you mean, you may know who did?"

"I saw a man with an ax."

"When?"

"Around three in the morning. Something like that. Maybe a little later. Maybe a little earlier."

"Go on," Reardon said.

"I was standing under the Delacorte animal clock.

You know, the one where the animal figures turn around when the clock chimes? You go under it to get to the Children's Zoo."

Reardon nodded.

"Well, I was standing in that little brick portal, and I saw a man pass me. He was wearing a Parks Department uniform. It was green. It said 'Parks Department' on the sleeve."

Reardon thought of Gilbert Noble. "Was the man you saw black or white?"

"He was white."

Reardon thought of Harry Bryant. "How big was he, the man in the uniform?"

"Average, I suppose. I'm almost six feet, and he was a lot shorter than me."

"Did you get a close look at this man?"

"Not at that point," Daniels said. "But later I got a good look."

"You saw him again?"

"Yes."

"How did you happen to see him again?"

"Well, he had only passed me a little while before when I started walking into the park in the same direction."

"Careful here," Mr. Tower whispered to Daniels.

"Yes, watch yourself," Mr. Arington said.

Daniels understood. "I mean, I was just strolling around. I wasn't looking for anything in particular. Like a connection, I mean. I wasn't looking for anything, any person." Daniels' fingers began to fidget nervously with the buttons of his shirt.

Reardon nodded. "I'm just interested in what you saw."

"I mean, the cops say I was going to meet a connection," blurted Daniels agitatedly. "For the cocaine they say I had."

"Just go ahead with the story," Mr. Tower said exasperatedly.

"As far as I'm concerned," Reardon said, "you were just taking a stroll in the park."

"Yeah, right," Daniels said. "A stroll. I strolled up the cement walk that leads from the animal clock to the Children's Zoo. That's where I saw the man again. I had a good look at him too. He looked strange. Kind of groggy. He looked so strange that I got a little scared, to tell you the truth. He looked like he was about ready to freak out. He was just leaning there against the deer cage, holding the ax."

"How did you know it was the deer cage?"

"Because I could see one of the deer peeking out of that tin house where they stay. Then this deer walked out toward the bars right up to the guy, poking its nose against his side, there where he was leaning."

"What happened then?"

"I just kept looking. Then he turned around and looked at me. But he didn't seem to see me. He was in a fog or something. Wacked out."

"Then what?" Reardon asked.

"He took a few steps away from the cage and just seemed to stand there, like he was in another world. Then he took a few more steps. That's when I got scared. Really scared. I started to walk away. Pretty fast too. I was afraid he was coming after me."

"Was he?"

"I thought so. So as I was walking, I looked back over my shoulder."

"And he wasn't following you?" Reardon asked.

"No. He had turned around again. He was walking away from me."

"Where was he walking to?"

Daniels smiled. "He was walking back toward the deer cage. He had taken the ax off his shoulder and was dragging it behind him, you know, like a kid would pull a wagon."

Reardon opened the top drawer of his desk and pulled out photographs of Gilbert Noble, Harry Bryant and Andros Petrakis. He laid the photos face up on the table and pushed them across the desk to Daniels. "Have you ever seen any of these men before?" he asked.

Daniels' face paled. "God, it scares me just looking at him," he muttered.

"Which one?"

He pointed to the photograph of Andros Petrakis, then stared up at Reardon. He grinned. "Bingo," he said.

16

So Harry Bryant had told the truth, Reardon thought, after Daniels and his attorneys had left the precinct house. Petrakis had come to work the night the fallow deer were killed. And Daniels had seen him there, slumped against the deer cage, a peculiar expression on his face, the ax nestled menacingly in his hands.

But Reardon was still no closer to Petrakis than the photograph he had already placed back in the top drawer of his desk. Petrakis and his whole family had vanished, leaving Reardon with nothing more than two conflicting images of the man. The one drawn by Mathesson was easier to understand. Mathesson had portrayed an enraged man, capable of sudden explosions of strength and violence, animated solely by an overwhelming hatred of Wallace Van Allen, who had come to symbolize for Petrakis the utter devastation of his life.

And so Andros Petrakis had killed. He had come at three in the morning from the deathbed of his wife to the Children's Zoo, where he began that process of revenge which, he believed, would result in the destruction of Wallace Van Allen. He had butchered a fallow deer with fifty-seven blows of an ax and killed the other with a single thrust. But that was only the beginning. He had then acquainted himself with Wallace Van Allen's holdings in New York. He had picked out an apartment house which belonged to Van Allen, waited patiently in the early hours of the morning, somehow managed to get into the apartment of Lee McDonald and Karen Ortovsky, and had then butchered them in exactly the same manner as the fallow deer.

Daniels had painted a different portrait, but Reardon could not get the lines and colors straight. The Petrakis that Daniels had seen leaning silently against the deer cage seemed a different sort of man from the one of Mathesson's narration. He had been leaning, simply leaning, on the cage with the ax nestled in his hands. That was what Reardon could not get out of his mind. That Petrakis had not been striding about menacingly tapping the ax blade against the bars but had been leaning like a tired workman against a wall, staring out into the dark air. And when one of the deer hesitantly moved toward the bars Petrakis had not jerked back but had continued to lean silently in the darkness while the fallow deer gently sniffed his trousers.

Reardon had seen murderous revenge. It did not lean silently in the early morning hours.

Who was Andros Petrakis, anyway? Reardon wondered.

Reardon had expected a long manhunt for Andros Petrakis, and so when he saw him for the first time only a few hours after Daniels and his lawyers had left the station house, he could not believe it. He looked up from his notes to rest his eyes and saw a small man in a green Parks Department uniform standing in front of the desk sergeant. Even in the distance there seemed to be something insubstantial about Petrakis. He stood before the large desk, staring up at Smith, waiting for some direction. Flooded by the light that flowed through the tall glass inlays of the precinct house doors, he looked more like an apparition than a man. The soiled uniform seemed to fall around him as if it were draped over a skeleton rather than a full-fleshed body. His arms hung loosely and motionlessly at his sides like those of a marionette.

Reardon waited, staring, unable to move. He saw Smith point in his direction and watched as Petrakis walked toward him.

Petrakis stopped directly in front of Reardon's desk and pointed to himself. "Petrakis," he said almost inaudibly.

Reardon stood up. "You are Andros Petrakis?"

"Andros Petrakis," the man repeated.

Reardon stared at him. He was about five-eight or nine but looked much smaller. He had a slight paunch, but even this characteristic only served to miniaturize him. The tiny, childlike face of Karen Ortovsky flashed through Reardon's mind. He blinked his eyes and tried to regain his concentration.

"Please sit down," Reardon said.

Nervously, Petrakis took a seat directly in front of Reardon's desk. He was very dark, with black curly hair and a thin mustache. A thick pungent odor surrounded him.

"Would you like a cup of coffee?"

"No," Petrakis said faintly. He seemed frail, lost, irredeemably abused.

"I understand that you recently lost your wife," Reardon said. "I'm sorry."

Petrakis nodded.

"My own wife died only a few weeks ago," Reardon added.

Petrakis said nothing, but his face took on a softness

that Reardon translated as an expression of understanding.

"We have been trying to find you," Reardon began.

Petrakis stared at Reardon without expression.

"Did you know that?" Reardon asked. "Did you know that the police wanted to talk to you?"

"I call Mr. Cohen. Try to get back work. He tell me come here."

"When did you talk to him?"

"Today. Just now."

"Do you know why we want to talk to you?"

Petrakis shrugged his shoulders.

"The deer," Reardon said. He looked for some response in Petrakis' face. He had seen people break down at the first mention of a crime which they alone knew they had committed. But Petrakis' face registered nothing.

"Have you spoken to anyone in the Parks Department besides Mr. Cohen?"

"No."

Reardon felt stymied. He had never seen a man so drained of concern or curiosity.

"Have you been to the park since early Sunday morning?" Reardon asked. He wanted to rivet Petrakis' attention on the fact that the police knew he had gone to the park that morning. Perhaps that would break him.

"No," Petrakis said.

"Are you sure?"

"Sure."

Reardon glanced down at his notes. He felt like a talk-show host without a guest. Petrakis sat directly in front of him, but no one really seemed to be there at all. Somehow he had to get at Petrakis, draw him out. He decided to be more direct.

"How long have you worked with the Parks Department?" he asked.

"Two years," Petrakis replied.

Dos, thought Reardon, and the roman numeral two. "You don't speak Spanish by any chance, do you, Mr. Petrakis?"

"Greek," Petrakis said.

Reardon looked down at his paper again. "Yes, I thought so. And you work with Gilbert Noble and Harry Bryant, is that right?"

Petrakis nodded.

The only part of Petrakis' body that had moved since the interrogation had begun, thought Reardon, was his head. "Let's get back to the deer." Reardon looked at Petrakis intently. There was no response. "Did you have much to do with the fallow deer? Did you tend to their cage?"

"Sometimes," Petrakis said, and for a moment he closed his eyes wearily, his head swaying very slightly forward and backward. But the face betrayed nothing, and Reardon was beginning to believe there was nothing for it to betray. "Sometimes you cleaned the cage and sometimes Bryant cleaned it and sometimes Noble cleaned it?" Petrakis made no response. Reardon decided to work on the details of what he already knew about Petrakis' home. Finally draw him out.

"On Monday, about three A.M., you met Harry Bryant in a coffee shop on Second Avenue, is that right?"

"Right," Petrakis replied.

"What did you talk about?"

"I move to a new place that Thursday."

"You moved from 109 East 90th Street?"

"Yes."

Reardon looked down at his notes. "What is your new address?"

"103 East 101st Street. My wife sister apartment. We move in with her. I have no money."

"You were evicted from your previous apartment?" Petrakis nodded.

"And who is the landlord of the building you had to leave?" Reardon asked, staring down at his notes as if it were just one more routine question.

"Robles," Petrakis said.

"He's your landlord?"

"He kick me out," Petrakis said without emotion.

"Do you know his first name?"

"He kick out a sick woman. He kick out my wife."

"Do you know his first name?" Reardon repeated.

"Julio," Petrakis said, "Julio Robles."

"Excuse me a moment, Mr. Petrakis." Reardon picked up the phone and called Mathesson. "Jack, I want you to go over to 109 East 90th Street and see if a Julio Robles is around. Mr. Petrakis says Robles is the landlord, so we could have made a mistake on the connection." Reardon hung up and glanced at Petrakis. "Sorry to interrupt," he said. But Petrakis seemed to have been unaware of or uninterested in the break-in time since the last question.

Reardon began again: "Did you have any kind of fight with this Julio Robles?"

"No."

"None at all?"

"No."

"When did you leave the coffee shop," Reardon asked. "About what time?"

"Ten minutes."

"Where did you go?"

"To work. The zoo."

"What happened when you got there?"

"I start to work."

"Doing what?"

Petrakis closed his eyes again and appeared to go far away.

"Doing what?" Reardon asked again.

"Cutting brush behind the shed."

"What shed?"

"The deer shed. The brush look bad."

"How did you cut the brush?"

"My ax."

A shiver went down Reardon's back. Could it be, Reardon wondered, that Petrakis would actually confess to the killing of the fallow deer in this blunt, dead monotone?

"And so you took the ax from the work shed and started to cut the brush?"

Petrakis nodded.

It was inconceivable, Reardon thought, that Petrakis had gone this far into an interrogation without discerning the reason for it. But he only said: "Then what?"

"I cut the brush. I think of my sick wife at home. I feel bad. My wife is sick."

"Yes," said Reardon, "go on."

"I cannot work. I think of my sick wife. Only my children are home."

"So what did you do?" Reardon asked.

"I cannot work," Petrakis said, "I go home."

"You went home? After coming that far?"

"Yes."

It could have happened, Reardon thought. He, himself, had come to work many times during Millie's illness and had then gotten sick with the pain of her dying and had gone home to see her and to be with her, to bring her what little comfort he could, while he

could. "What did you do with the ax? Did you put it
back in the shed?"

"No, put it down," Petrakis said.

"Where?"

"By the deer cage," Petrakis said.

"And then you went home?"

"Yes."

"To East 101st Street?"

"Yes."

"What did you do when you got home?"

"I go to sleep."

"Did you go out again during the night?" Reardon
asked.

"No."

This was going nowhere, Reardon knew. He had to
get to the point quickly, flush Petrakis out, hit him
hard. "You said that you don't know why the police
were looking for you. Well, the reason is: the fallow
deer, the ones whose cage you sometimes cleaned,
were killed early Monday morning."

Petrakis received this information without any sign
of emotion. He seemed to project only a dull acknowl-
edgment of yet another insignificant fact.

"Were you aware that they had been killed?" Reardon asked.

"No."

"You would have noticed that they were dead when
you came to the park, wouldn't you?"

"They alive."

"And you say you placed your ax outside the cage
when you left the park. Why didn't you lock it up?"

"Too tired," Petrakis said. "I put it down and leave."

Reardon nodded. Then he said sternly, almost accusingly, "Your ax was the weapon that killed the fallow
deer."

Petrakis was unmoved. He simply nodded, staring dreamingly into Reardon's face.

"Your fingerprints are the only fingerprints on the ax," Reardon said in the same commanding voice.

Petrakis did not answer.

"Have you ever heard of Wallace Van Allen?" Reardon asked.

"He gives the deer to the zoo," Petrakis said.

"And he threw you out of your apartment too," Reardon said, "didn't he?"

"No," Petrakis said. "Robles."

"Wallace Van Allen owns the building," Reardon said.

"Oh," Petrakis said.

"You knew that, didn't you?"

"No."

"And you hated him, didn't you? Didn't you want to get even?"

Petrakis did not answer.

"Didn't you?" Reardon repeated.

Petrakis' face seemed to darken. "It is the curse," he said. "I will die!"

Reardon leaned forward in his chair. For a moment he believed that he had broken the impenetrable surface of Petrakis' consciousness. "Die for what?"

"This is the last," Petrakis said.

"Last of what?"

"The curse."

"What curse?"

"She curses me with three deaths."

"Who?"

"My mother."

"Why?"

"Because I leave my village in Greece. She says three would die."

"She cursed you for coming to New York?" Reardon asked. He had heard of such things among the Irish.

Petrakis continued, dazed. "She says that three will die. My daughter last year. Now my wife. Now me."

"Your daughter died last year?" Reardon asked.

"Born dead," Petrakis said without emphasis, as if filling in an inconsequential detail, as if all his nerves had been seared down to a final insensibility.

Reardon could feel a pressure behind his eyes, his skin tightening in the old, remembered fury of his pity.

17

Reardon was still questioning Petrakis, searching for contradictions, breaks, discrepancies in his story when Mathesson walked into the precinct house later that afternoon. He seemed to be moved by a dynamo, gaining energy from the pursuit of the killer. Reardon could sense that Mathesson smelled blood, felt he was on the right track and had already fingered Petrakis as the killer in his mind. He looked at Petrakis, then at Reardon. "Can I see you a minute?" he asked Reardon.

Reardon stood up, and he and Mathesson walked into an empty office not far from Reardon's desk. Mathesson was poised, ready. He paced to the back wall of the office, leaned his back flat against it and slapped his hands together jubilantly.

"The Van Allen connection still checks out," he said. "Julio Robles is just the lousy superintendent of the building. He's not the landlord."

"Van Allen is the landlord?"

"That's right," Mathesson said, "and I did a little survey. You know, on my own. Everybody in that building that I could talk to knew that Wallace Van Allen was the landlord."

Reardon nodded. There was no doubt now, Reardon knew: Mathesson was after Petrakis and already believed he had him.

"It was just like I thought," Mathesson said, "just like my buddy with the Hollywood star for a landlord."

169

"I see," Reardon said.

"So the connection holds."

"Yes, I guess it does."

"You gonna arrest him?" Mathesson asked. "Got a lot on him, you know."

Reardon looked at Petrakis through the internal office window. He was sitting erect in the chair, his hands folded motionlessly in his lap, his face still holding to its doomed rigidity, the face of a cow waiting for the hammer.

"He says he crossed Fifth Avenue on the way to the subway," Reardon said.

"Then that's it," said Mathesson. "Piccolini wants an arrest."

"I know."

"Do you think you can get a confession out of Petrakis?"

"Like they got one out of Whitmore," Reardon said harshly, "by feeding him the details of the case." He felt his anger flash almost uncontrollably. He gazed at Petrakis, thinking of that impregnable passivity the man gave off like an odor. "They actually got him to tell them the color of a bedspread in a murder room he had never been in," Reardon said softly, controlling himself. "That's not the kind of confession we want, is it?"

"Of course not," Mathesson said. "You know better than that. You know I wouldn't go for anything like that."

"If I build a case against Petrakis," Reardon said, "I want it to stick. Besides, I'm not sure we have a case yet."

Mathesson seemed amazed. "Are you kidding?"

"I have an opinion," Reardon said firmly, turning

to face Mathesson, "and that's it. I don't believe we have a case nailed down against him yet."

"The connection holds, the prints hold, the motive holds, the weapon holds. He was in the area of the crime near the time of its commission."

Reardon thought Mathesson sounded like a textbook on criminal procedure.

"I'm not convinced."

Mathesson's initial amazement was obviously now turning into irritation. "Are you going on hunches now?"

"You can call it what you like." Reardon pointed his finger toward the closed door. "Outside that door a man is sitting in a chair. That man is a part of this case. He's a part of this case, just like the ax and the prints and the rest of the physical evidence. He just does not connect with the facts. I don't believe the case is solid against him and I am not going to subject him and his family to an arrest before I have a case I can send to court."

"Is that what you're going to say to Piccolini?"

"That is just about it."

"Forget it," Mathesson said wearily. "Petrakis will be in the slammer tonight no matter what. Piccolini won't buy any of this."

"Maybe so," Reardon said.

"For sure," Mathesson said. "And I'll tell you something, John. I don't buy it either. You've gone a little crazy on this case. Don't ask me why, but you've been a little crazy on it from the beginning, from the first day when you saw those deer. And you're going to fuck yourself up royally. And it's all going to be for nothing. For that little shit out there. Who cares about him? He did it. Everything connects. I believe he did it. And I hope to hell that Piccolini locks him up, because he may have wasted more than those deer. He may have wasted two women in the Village. Remember, the one with the face like a child? I don't want him on the streets because you have a hunch he didn't do it."

For a moment Mathesson glared furiously at Reardon, then he strode out of the office, slamming the door behind him.

Reardon, exhausted, sat down in the empty office at the empty desk, the light streaming through the window, illuminating cascading clouds of city dust, alone.

When Reardon emerged from the office he walked directly past Petrakis and straight to Piccolini's office. He entered it without knocking and closed the door behind him. Piccolini's head shot up, startled. But when he saw Reardon standing stiffly in front of his desk, he relaxed, placed a hand behind his head and leaned back in his chair. He smiled. "Finished?"

"I don't think so," Reardon said.

"What's the problem? Have you finished the interrogation?"

"Just about."

"Did he confess?"

"No."

Piccolini smiled. "He will," he said confidently. "Maybe not right away, but he will."

"No," Reardon said, "he won't."

"It doesn't matter anyway, does it?"

"Well . . ."

"Just go over the basics again," Piccolini said.

"Well," Reardon said, "we found the weapon. A Parks Department ax. Only one set of fingerprints; they belong to Petrakis. According to Daniels, Petrakis was near the Children's Zoo just before the deer were killed. He was mad at his landlord, according to Bryant. His landlord was Wallace Van Allen. Petrakis knew the deer were given to the zoo by Van Allen because he worked there when they were donated."

"Did you confront him with those facts?" Piccolini asked.

"Yes."

"And he didn't confess?"

"No."

"Arrest him," Piccolini said matter-of-factly.

"No," Reardon said. "I don't think we have a complete case."

"Why not?"

"I just don't believe we do."

Piccolini leaned forward in his chair and folded his hands in front of him. "That's it? That's your whole explanation?"

"Yes."

"Based on nothing."

"Based on Petrakis. I don't believe he connects with the facts of the case."

"He connects with the physical evidence," Piccolini said, "and that's enough of a connection for me. Arrest him." He turned casually to get a book from the shelf behind his desk.

"No," Reardon said, his whole body growing taut.

Piccolini wheeled around to face Reardon. "Arrest him!" he said coldly.

"Have him arrested if you want to, but not by me. I won't do it. Get somebody else, not me."

"Petrakis had a motive for the crime and the occasion to commit it," Piccolini insisted.

"What motive?"

"What motive?" Piccolini said. "Are you kidding? He was in a rage at his landlord and his landlord was

Wallace Van Allen. That's a motive in anybody's book."

Reardon shrugged. "Petrakis thought his landlord was Julio Robles."

"Who is Julio Robles?"

"The super in Petrakis' old building."

Piccolini grinned. "That's just a cover. I've heard stuff like that a thousand times. So have you."

"I believe he did not know that Wallace Van Allen owned the building he lived in," Reardon said.

Piccolini leaned back in his chair. "I don't know what's the matter with you, Reardon, but something is."

Reardon said nothing. He was not sure he disagreed with Piccolini about that. He was not sure but that something terrible was in fact wrong with him, but he could not name it.

"Do you have any real reason to hold off on the arrest of Petrakis?" Piccolini asked.

"No," Reardon said immediately.

"Then arrest him."

"No."

"You're off the case," Piccolini said abruptly. "Send Mathesson in here. And tell Petrakis to wait right where he is."

Reardon nodded. He felt like Petrakis. He felt as though there was nothing left of him.

That night Reardon could not sleep. He sat by his window watching the life of the street coil and strike beneath him. His mind was filled with the grotesque opera of his life: the hideous dismemberments, the familiar molestations. He remembered Whitmore, a confused and lonely boy from whom the detectives had gently nudged a false confession the way a kindly grandparent might coax candy from a grandchild. That's what Mathesson and the others will do to Petrakis, he thought. Piccolini was right: Petrakis would confess to everything. He would embrace a confession as the fulfillment of his mother's curse.

Reardon shook his head. He was off the case. He had been reassigned. It was his duty to take the reassignment, to forget about Petrakis, to let Mathesson and Piccolini handle it. Tomorrow morning there would be another homicide. The city offered up unexplained corpses with every dawn.

World without end, amen.

18

TUESDAY

Toward dawn the walls of Reardon's apartment seemed to be closing in on him. He had smoked three packs of cigaretes since eight o'clock, and the room floated before him in a haze of smoke. He crushed out the last cigarette of the third pack and walked down to the street.

Outside the early-morning delivery trucks lined the streets and avenues. The veins of the city were receiving their daily injections of food and drink and produce. The delivery men hustled from their trucks to the stores and back to the trucks again. It seemed to Reardon that they purposely made as much noise as possible, banging their carts on the curb or letting their packages drop from shoulder height to the sidewalk.

At 86th Street he took the Lexington Avenue express uptown toward the Bronx, something he often did when he felt the need for escape. Soon the train came out of the subway tunnel's grimy darkness, and he was in open air again. From the tracks he could see the streets below him, but the sounds of the city were distant, less threatening, muffled by the whirr of the train. From the el the world seemed small and salvageable. The complexities of the city, its sprawling, unmanageable life, were reduced to a miniature version of itself.

177

All its problems, and all of his, appeared less colossal from the vantage point of the train.

For years it had been Reardon's final escape. It took him above everything, above the bickerings of family life, the rigors of work, the austerities of religion. It was the place where he regained himself, calmed himself, somehow took on the armor of endurance.

Between the Burnside Avenue and 183rd Street stations the train suddenly stopped. After a few moments the conductor announced over the public address system that there was a train out of service up ahead and that there would be a short delay. Reardon took the delay as a gift, a moment simply to rest, suspended between the city and the sky.

His eyes patrolled the windows that faced him on the other side of the tracks, probably only fifty feet away. The building was old and weather-beaten, but the apartment windows were large and full. Curtains or venetian blinds covered most of them, so Reardon's eyes fastened onto the one window open to his view. He could see a man pacing in a circle around a small boy. The man was dressed in work clothes and was very animated, throwing his arms in the air as he circled the child. Then he hit him, hard, with his open hand, and the child fell back into a chair.

Reardon stood up, astonished, and bolted across the center aisle to the subway window.

The man was shouting, but Reardon could not hear what he was saying. The man picked up a large vase and threw it across the room. The child darted behind the chair and squatted, and Reardon could see that he was covering his head with his tiny arms. Instantly the man wrenched the child from behind the chair and lifted him into the air above his head.

Reardon frantically tried to get the subway window open, but the latches were corroded shut.

The man threw the boy into the back of the chair, toppling it so that it spilled the child onto the floor.

Reardon began hitting the window with his fists again and again. "Stop it! Stop it!" he shouted. The other passengers in the train turned to look at him, and then at the scene in the apartment. But their attention returned to him, as if he were the greater threat.

The man picked the boy up again and slapped him across the room. Then he caught him by the collar and threw him across the legs of the toppled chair. The boy jumped to his feet and ran to a corner of the room, out of Reardon's sight. The man began to walk slowly toward the corner.

Reardon's knuckles were stiff and reddened; he stopped hitting the glass and stood trembling by the window.

The train jerked forward. Reardon's eyes burned into the apartment window, but he could see nothing except the legs of the overturned chair, the jagged glass dotting the floor and the blank wall that stood behind it all, featureless and resolute, like a pitiless, refusing hand.

When the train reached 183rd Street, Reardon got off and called the local precinct to report what he had seen. He did not expect much action to be taken. He could not be that specific as to the location of the building, and he was unable to give a close, detailed description of either the man or the child.

"Thank you, Detective Reardon," the desk sergeant at the precinct house said. "We'll look into it."

"I hope so," Reardon replied, but he knew that the

incident would not get a high priority. He had not even been asked to accompany a patrol car to find the building where he had seen the child beaten.

He took the same train back to Manhattan, but it passed the window so fast that he could not see anything in the room. The light was still on; that was all that he could tell.

He got off the train at 86th Street and walked to his apartment. The city was coming to life. Some people, Reardon knew, would not be around to see it. Some would be stuffed in car trunks. Others would be hanging in closets. Still others would be floating in bathtubs filled with blood and torn flesh. Mathesson had once referred to such a scene as "Manhattan clam chowder."

Reardon wondered about the boy he had seen through the window. He thought of the tiny arms folded around the head. Perhaps, Reardon thought, that was the only appropriate posture for this world. In Catholicism, Reardon knew, there were two unforgivable sins: one of them was despair. Standing on the sidewalk amid the early-morning jostling of pedestrians, his shoulders hunched and combative, his face locked in an animal grimace, Reardon suspected that he might be edging toward the unforgivable.

19

When Reardon got to the precinct house later that morning, Mathesson met him at his desk. He stood hesitantly for a moment, as if waiting for the bustle of the precinct house to die down. Then he offered Reardon a slight smile.

"You're back on the case," he said.

"What?"

Mathesson's eyes roamed over Reardon's face and body. "Jesus, you look busted," he said.

"What about the case?"

"You're back on it."

"Why?"

Mathesson stepped aside to allow Reardon to get to the chair behind his desk.

"Well, looks like Piccolini overstepped his authority a little, the prick. He got his ass chewed out. Downtown told that little dago they'd decide when you were off the case." Mathesson smirked. "That little prick is just a paper pusher, and they know that downtown. He's just a paper pusher; he don't break cases. He don't do anything." Mathesson grinned. "Well, he got the shit kicked out of him this time."

"What about Petrakis?" Reardon asked.

"What about him?"

"Where is he?"

"In the clink."

"He was arrested?"

"Damn right," Mathesson said. "I arrested him, my-self, but it's gonna go out as a real team effort."

"Go out?"

"Haven't you read the paper this morning?"

"No," Reardon said.

Mathesson took a *Daily News* from under his arm and gave it to Reardon.

The whole story was there. The killing of the fallow deer, the investigation, and the arrest of the alleged perpetrator: Andros Petrakis. On the front page, di-dectly under the headline, "Arrest in Deerslaying Case," there were large full-scale photographs of Wallace, Melinda and Dwight Van Allen. On the in-side there was a photo spread of the fallow deer cage, the entrance to the Children's Zoo and the apartment building in which the Van Allens lived. There was also a picture of Reardon himself. In small type, under Reardon's photograph, the copy read: "Detective John Reardon headed investigation which led to arrest." There was a picture of the evening press conference at which the Police Commissioner had announced the breaking of the case. And in the right-hand corner there was a small photograph of Andros Petrakis.

"Did you meet the Van Allen kids?" Mathesson asked.

"One of them."

"Twins," Mathesson said.

"Yes, I know," Reardon said indifferently. He stared at the pictures of the Van Allen family.

"That Melinda's not a bad-looking girl," Mathesson said.

Reardon remembered the rather tall, slightly over-weight, generally unattractive young woman who had so annoyed and befuddled him a week before. "Not bad," he said. He looked at Mathesson. "She has a kind face."

Reardon's first act after being reinstated on the case was to visit Petrakis at the Tombs, even though he dreaded seeing him there. If the precinct house had reduced Petrakis to a kind of gelatinous inactivity, he could only imagine what the grinding oppressiveness of the Tombs would do to him. It had been well named, Reardon thought, this prison of the City of New York; it was a place for the dead.

Petrakis was led out by a guard and seated at a table opposite Reardon. He had not changed much, Reardon saw instantly. The face retained its motionless, stony aspect, the eyes staring rigidly ahead but seeming to comprehend nothing beyond them—not movement or person or meaning.

"Have you contacted your family?" Reardon asked.

"No," Petrakis said dully. He did not seem to see Reardon at all, but only to look through him, as if he were a ghost.

"Why not? Won't they worry about you, about where you are?"

"I tell them I not come back," Petrakis said in the same granite monotone of the precinct house.

"When?"

"Before I come to police."

All around them there was sound and movement. Prisoners and their visitors were filing in and out amid a humming welter of hellos and good-byes, but Petrakis did not seem to be aware of any of it. It was as if he had closed himself up in a box of his own making and had sealed all its cracks from light and sound.

"Mr. Petrakis, did you kill those deer in the Children's Zoo?"

"I will die for it," Petrakis said.

"Killing animals is not a capital offense in New York State," Reardon said, "or any place else I know of. You can't be executed for that."

"Then something else," Petrakis said.

Instantly Reardon thought of the Village murders. "Have you ever heard the names Karen Ortovsky or Lee McDonald?" he asked.

"No."

"Do you ever go to Greenwich Village?"

"No."

Reardon could never remember having felt such exasperation. There was life all around them, even in the intolerable hurt and confinement of the Tombs. But Petrakis' heart seemed to beat beneath a breast of stone.

"Have you done anything that is punishable by death in this state?" Reardon asked.

Petrakis stared straight ahead. "I do not obey my mother."

"Besides that."

"That is enough."

"But besides that," Reardon insisted.

"No."

Reardon stood up. "I think you should call your family and let them know where you are. If you want, I will call them for you."

"They know where I am," Petrakis said.

"They know where you are?"

"Dead," Petrakis said.

Reardon took one of his cards and placed it carefully on the table in front of Petrakis. "Call me if you need anything, or if anything comes to you that can shed some light on this case."

Petrakis said nothing.

"Will you call me?" Reardon asked.

"I am dead," Petrakis said.

"Not yet, Mr. Petrakis," Reardon said, "not yet."

When he reached the door Reardon turned to watch Petrakis disappear behind the door that led to the cells. He glanced at the table where he and Petrakis had talked. His card rested faceup on the table like a corpse on a mortuary slab.

Driving back to the precinct house, Reardon felt the case of the fallow deer plummeting toward him like a bird of prey. He believed Petrakis could be convicted for the killing of the deer on the evidence already assembled. He knew how it would go in the courtroom. Witnesses could place Petrakis at the deer cage with an ax in his hand only moments before they were killed. Bryant would testify that Petrakis was highly agitated, even furious, when he had met him in the coffee shop the morning the fallow deer were killed. On the witness stand Daniels would paint a sinister portrait of Petrakis, one which would doubtless chill the nerves of the jury; the district attorney's office might even give Daniels a break on the cocaine bust if his testimony was convincing enough. The ax itself would be displayed before the jury, complete with bloodstains. It would be pointed out that Petrakis' fingerprints were all over it. Worst of all, Reardon knew, Petrakis would probably confess. He had seen far stronger suspects crumble under grueling interrogation. And Petrakis already seemed beyond caring whether he was guilty or not.

But there were still the murders of Lee McDonald and Karen Ortovsky. So far the only thing that could connect Petrakis with their deaths was Mathesson's revenge theory. Reardon knew that still left a lot to be explained. Why were the deer and the women killed in exactly the same way with fifty-seven blows on one body and only one on the other? And what did the roman numeral "two" and "dos" mean?

Reardon was certain that the deer and the women had been killed by the same person. The deer investigation seemed at a dead end. But the case of McDonald and Ortovsky still had one line of investigation open: Jamie O'Rourke.

Reardon stopped for a traffic light and glanced through his notebook for O'Rourke's address. When he had found it he turned his car around and headed toward the Brooklyn Bridge.

Time was what he did not have much of, and he felt its movement take an enormous wave thundering toward shore.

Jamie O'Rourke lived in a Brooklyn row house on a street of Brooklyn row houses, drab, featureless, decaying like a dead body in a warm room. Reardon had seen these neighborhoods before, always feeling that somehow an immense and secret crime had been committed against the residents. They lived like citizens of a besieged city, in constant dread of invasion by any people different from themselves—non-Catholics, nonwhites, both, anything.

He climbed the steps to the door of O'Rourke's house and rang the bell. He heard slight movements within the house but no one came to the door. He rang again.

This time the door opened. "If you're a Jehovah's Witness selling God, I ain't buying none," said a man dressed in dark-blue pants and a T-shirt, a bathroom towel wrapped loosely around his neck.

Reardon showed his gold shield. "My name is Reardon," he said.

"What do you want?" the man asked harshly. He swabbed the back of his neck with the towel and looked suspiciously at Reardon.

"Are you Jamie O'Rourke?" Reardon asked.

"That's right."

"I understand you were married to Patty McDonald."

The man pulled the towel from around his neck and wiped his hands. "You think I killed her?"

"I'm trying to find out who did," Reardon said.

"I don't know nothing about her," O'Rourke said sharply. "She run out on me a long time ago. I ain't seen her."

"You were at her funeral."

O'Rourke looked at Reardon warily. "Well, I got a right to go to her funeral, don't I? She was my wife."

"I'm not here to cause you trouble," Reardon said.

"I'm not afraid of trouble."

"Well, maybe you wouldn't mind talking to me about her then."

O'Rourke wiped his face with the towel. "I was just shaving," he said. "I got to go to work tonight."

"It won't take long."

O'Rourke studied Reardon's face, came to some conclusion about him, and opened the door wider. "Come on in then."

Inside Reardon quietly viewed the disarray around him. The room was furnished with an overstuffed sofa and two chairs, a heavy coffee table and matching end table. The stuffing of the couch was easily visible through gaping rents in the fabric. The coffee table was spotted with water stains and scarred as if raked with a fork. Sheets of floral wallpaper barely hung from the walls, and leaks had caused yellowed paint to peel halfway across the ceiling. There were no curtains; the venetian blinds which afforded some privacy hung askew from dirty windows. The only signs of habitation were old copies of the *Daily News* piled on chairs and the floor and four or five crushed Schlitz cans.

"Sit down anywhere," O'Rourke said. He looked around the room as if disgusted with it himself. "My old man told me I didn't give a shit for nothing. That was the only truth that old man ever told me."

Reardon grabbed a handful of newspapers from a chair and deposited them on a nearby table. "I'll just sit here," he said.

"Suit yourself," O'Rourke said. He plopped down on the tattered sofa across from Reardon and stared at him silently, waiting.

Reardon pulled out his notebook and removed a ballpoint from his shirt pocket.

"You Irish?" O'Rourke asked suddenly.

Reardon nodded.

"From Brooklyn?"

Reardon shook his head. "Bronx. University Avenue around Fordham Road."

O'Rourke grinned. "Jesus Christ, you might as well have been born in the Vatican."

Reardon smiled. "Father Zeiser Place, actually."

O'Rourke smiled widely. "Good God, how come you ain't a priest?"

"Everybody else was," Reardon said.

"I'd offer you something to eat," O'Rourke said, "but I don't keep no food in the house. Brings rats." He glanced about the room again. "I know what you must think of this place, but just remember, if you think I like it, you're wrong."

"I've seen worse."

"You've probably seen blood all over the walls," O'Rourke said darkly.

"Sometimes."

O'Rourke took a handkerchief from his back pocket and blew his nose. "I have a cold all winter," he explained as he returned the handkerchief to his pocket. "I work as a night watchman in this old warehouse on Flatbush Avenue. They got this one little heater for the whole place. So I'm sick all the time."

Beneath the worn, lined face Reardon could see that O'Rourke remained a young man, prematurely aging, strained and slowly breaking under the load.

"Well, I guess you got some questions to ask," O'Rourke said, "so go ahead. I got to be at the warehouse in an hour."

Looking at O'Rourke, Reardon sensed something that he believed was important, sensed that O'Rourke might understand the troubles of Andros Petrakis and offer across the great distance that divided them some element of concern. He decided to take a chance.

"I'm going to lay it on the line for you," he said. "They've got a guy in the Tombs, and they're going to try to pin the double murder on him." Reardon looked intently into O'Rourke's face. "I don't think he's the one."

O'Rourke raised himself up slightly from his slumped position on the sofa.

"They arrested him for something else," Reardon said, "for another crime. But I think they'll try to get him for killing Patty and her roommate too. I don't think he committed any of these crimes, Mr. O'Rourke."

O'Rourke's face hardened. "What's this guy do?"

"He worked in the Parks Department, cleaning up the animal cages, things like that."

"That's a shit job," O'Rourke said. "And they're trying to lay a murder rap on him?"

"Yes."

"That stinks," O'Rourke said. "That really stinks."

"Yes, it does, Mr. O'Rourke," Reardon said quietly.

"What makes them think he did it?"

"They have some evidence," Reardon said. "But I don't believe any of it. I've met the man. I don't think he could have done it. He's too worn out. It takes a lot of energy to kill."

O'Rourke pulled himself erect on the sofa and planted his feet on the floor. "How can I help?"

"I'm not sure you can," Reardon told him, "but I think the only way I can get him off is to find out who killed Patty and her roommate. You see, whoever did that did the other thing too. The one the guy is charged with."

"I know what you mean," O'Rourke said. "I'll do whatever I can. Ask me anything. If it takes a long time, tough shit. There ain't nothing in that warehouse anybody wants anyway."

Reardon looked closely at O'Rourke. "How long were you married to Patty?"

"Four years. That's how long we lived together. We're still married. Never did get no divorce."

"Four years," Reardon repeated.

"That's right," O'Rourke said, "and not a good year among them, to tell you the truth. She was sixteen years old when I married her. Just a little girl really. Beautiful too."

"That's young to marry," Reardon coaxed.

"Yeah, it's young. But if you lived with Sam Mc-Donald you'd of married young too. That's her father." O'Rourke's eyes narrowed spitefully. "He's a brutal bastard. Used to beat the shit out of his wife, the fucking pig. Used to beat the shit out of Patty too."

Reardon nodded.

"Patty was an only child," O'Rourke continued. "You know why?"

Reardon shook his head.

" 'Cause his wife couldn't have no more children, 'cause she was carrying another baby, would have been Patty's brother or sister, and he beat his wife up and she had a miscarriage, and she couldn't have no more children after that." O'Rourke sneered. "He's a good Catholic, ain't he? Just about lives in the confessional over at Saint Jude's. Well, he's got a lot to confess, but if I had any say in it, Sam McDonald would roast in hell."

"Was there an investigation of that beating?"

"Who would testify against him? A little five-year-old girl like Patty was when it happened? His wife? Mary McDonald wouldn't testify against her husband if he roasted her on a skewer."

Reardon recognized that none of this had much to do with the case. But sometimes people had to be allowed to talk, to ramble, to work up to the relevant issue. By the time they got there, Reardon knew, they would be ready, and nothing could hold them back.

"Naw, hell," O'Rourke said with disgust, "old Sam probably gave her a little peck on the cheek and whispered a *mea culpa* or two and that was the end of it." His face saddened and his voice became abruptly softer. "Well, I learned something from Sam McDonald," he said. "I learned what beating up on people leads to. And I'll tell you something, I never hurt Patty. I never laid a hand on her. We had our troubles, who don't? And she left me. Happens to a lot of people. But I never hurt her, never hit her or anything like that. Fact is, I loved that little girl. Problem was, she didn't stay little. She was smart as a whip. Read all the time. I'm not that way at all. Just a dumb Brooklyn mick, that's me. A working stiff. But I loved her, and I never hurt her. I don't have to crawl over to Saint Jude's every fifteen minutes confessing about all the people I've destroyed. Not like Sam."

"Did Patty have any friends in Brooklyn? People she stayed in contact with after she moved to Manhattan?"

O'Rourke shook his head. "She said good riddance to everything and everybody in Brooklyn. Myself included."

"No one at all?" Reardon asked again. "This could be important."

"I'd like to help, but she left Brooklyn for good. She didn't have nobody but me here anyway. She didn't have no friends. She used to just sit in this front room and stare out the window. I'd come home. I had a day job then. I'd come home, drive up out there, and there she'd be. Curled up in that little chair you're sitting in, staring out the window, just like a cat. No expression on her face. Just staring like she was watching a boring movie or something."

"How often did you see her after she left?"

"Not much. It's like she built a wall around herself. I'd see her once in a while. I'd try to be friendly. I'd say, 'What's new?' or 'What you been up to?'—things like that. And she'd just say, 'I'm okay, I guess,' and that'd be the end of it."

"She never mentioned anyone she knew there?"

"No, not that I can recall."

"Never?"

"I don't think so," O'Rourke said. "I know it's strange. I thought so at the time. But I figured she just didn't want me to know anything about her, wanted me to keep my nose out of her life. Well, I figured if that's what she wants that's what I'll do. So after a while we just talked about nothing whenever we saw each other: movies, TV, shit like that. Nothing personal."

"Did you ever visit her in her apartment in Manhattan?"

O'Rourke's eyes widened. "Oh, no," he said, "that was impossible. She was very strict about that. I never saw where she lived. The whole four years she was in Manhattan I was never up to her place." O'Rourke looked embarrassed. "I know I must sound like a jerk to you, seeing somebody that long that wouldn't even let me in the front door, but I couldn't help it." O'Rourke's voice tightened. "Fact is, I couldn't leave it alone. I kept loving her. Ain't that goofy?"

"No," Reardon said quietly.

"I look around this place sometimes," O'Rourke said gently, "and I remember what it was like when she was here. The worst of it was better than this shit."

Reardon nodded.

"You married?" O'Rourke asked.

"I was," Reardon said. "My wife died."

"Sorry to hear it."

Reardon nodded. "Do you think Mr. McDonald could have done anything to Patty?"

O'Rourke looked at Reardon with surprise. "You mean kill her? No, he's a rotten bastard, a real pig, but he couldn't do that."

"You have any idea at all who might have done such a thing?"

"No. I wish to hell I did. I'd break his fucking back

if I caught him. Maybe she had some enemies in Manhattan. I wouldn't know about that. Or maybe they came after the other one, the roommate, or maybe it was just some crazy man."

"Why did you stop seeing Patty?"

"That's the way she wanted it," O'Rourke said. "She said she was starting a new life."

"What did she mean?"

O'Rourke smiled. "I've heard lots of people say that and I never saw it mean anything at all."

"She didn't tell you anything about what she meant?"

"Yeah," O'Rourke said. "She told me, or tried to. I couldn't make much sense out of it."

"What did she say?"

"She said a friend of hers and her was going to get out of the States," O'Rourke said. "She said she couldn't take it here anymore. Maybe Sam was bothering her again, maybe some boyfriend dumped on her, I don't know. Anyway, she had some shit left in the house here and she wanted to come and get it. She wanted to sell it. She was trying to get the money together to go to Europe and live. Her and her friend were going together."

"Was that Karen Ortovsky?" Reardon asked.

"She never mentioned a name."

"Did she say anything else?"

"Yeah," O'Rourke said weakly. "Yeah, she hit me with the divorce stuff. But I just couldn't do it. I must of been crazy to say no to her about that. I ain't religious. I didn't give a shit what the Church said. But somehow I just couldn't get it into my damn head that she was never going to come back to me." O'Rourke waved one arm across the room. "Never going to come back to this," he said with a painful laugh.

"So you refused to give her a divorce?" Reardon said.

O'Rourke stared at Reardon. "She got real mad about that," he said softly. "She abused me a little, to tell you the truth. When I heard her I knew it was the last time we'd ever have a friendly word with each other. We were in a coffee shop. She just seemed to blow up, and I just sat there listening to her. She was calling me all kinds of names. I'd never heard that kind of stuff come out of her mouth. I must of been in shock. I couldn't say nothing back. If a guy on the job called me those names I'd break his goddamn neck. But I just sat there like a stupid ass. Then she just stopped. She just looked at me for a long time without saying nothing. Then she got up and walked out. And I came home. And you know what I did?"

Reardon shook his head. He wondered how long O'Rourke had held this hurt mutely within him. He felt like the whiskey priest who waits and listens, but who knows that in the end he will have no balm to offer.

"I guess you noticed I'm a big guy?"

"Yes."

"Well, I came home and for the next two hours I tore this fucking house apart. That's why it looks like this. I turned over everything. I ripped off the wallpaper. I pulled down the shelves that were on the wall. And I ain't fixed nothing yet." He paused, breathing heavily. His face was flushed. Slowly he regained control of himself. "When I was finished, when there was nothing else to rip up or tear down, I curled up on this sofa and I cried like a baby until morning. If I hadn't had a job to go to the next day I think I would have killed myself."

"And you never saw her or heard from her again?" Reardon asked.

O'Rourke shook his head. "No, I never did," he said. "Heard from a guy said he was her lawyer, but never from her."

"A lawyer?" Reardon asked.

"Yeah," O'Rourke said contemptuously. "Some bastard called me the next day. Said he was representing Lee McDonald. He said I had to give her a divorce, and if I didn't he'd drag me into court and smear my name all over New York—sue me for everything I had, get me fired from my job, all that shit. He was a real nasty bastard."

"Did you ever meet him?"

"Hell, no," O'Rourke said angrily. "I told him he could go fuck himself. I told him if he ever came anywhere near me I'd tear his head off. I never heard from him again."

"Did he tell you his name?"

"Yeah."

"Do you remember it?"

"I never forgot anything that had to do with Patty."

Reardon took out his notebook. "What was his name?"

"Phillip Cardan," O'Rourke said.

20

Names, Reardon knew, led to other names. Father Perry had led to Jamie O'Rourke. Now Jamie O'Rourke had led to someone called Phillip Cardan. Cardan had represented himself as a lawyer, but Reardon could not be sure that was true. It would be easy enough to find out; the Yellow Pages under attorneys might be enough. But Reardon decided to try something else first.

Back at his desk in the precinct he picked up the phone and dialed the number of the law firm where Lee McDonald had worked for the last five years before her death.

"Bailey, Merritt and White," a female voice answered.

"May I speak to Mr. Phillip Cardan, please," Reardon said.

"Just a moment, please."

Reardon waited, feeling the pressures of passing time, knowing that Petrakis was not safe in prison, that no one was safe in the Tombs, least of all an unstable middle-aged family man who had never been forcibly detained in his life.

Finally the voice returned to the line. "Mr. Cardan is out of the office at the moment. We expect him to return at approximately four-thirty. May I take a message?"

Reardon looked at his watch. It was four fifteen.

"Any message?" the voice repeated.

"Yes, thank you," Reardon said. "Would you tell him that John Reardon called? I'm with the New York City Police Department." Reardon gave the woman his number. "Have him call me as soon as possible," he said, and hung up.

It was the first break, Reardon recognized. Lee McDonald had confided something to someone. That was a beginning. He could not guess where it might lead.

He stood up and walked to the front of the precinct house. Outside a gray bleakness was tightening in on the city like a constricting serpent. The last mildness of fall would soon be lost, and after that the relentless cold and frigid careering winds would drive the people from the streets and parks.

It would be his first Christmas without Millie. Tim and Abbey would try futilely to make up for her absence. They would bring expensive gifts that he did not want and could not use. They would bring him a case of Irish whiskey when a fifth would do. They would try to be jolly, as the season required.

He opened the door and stepped out into the street. Toward the end of the block he could see a group of young people slouching against a car. They were giggling and poking each other playfully. For a moment, he felt an intense desire to join them, to stroll over to where they were, buy them all a slice of pizza, and there, in the casual warmth of the pizza parlor, tell them all he had seen and felt and learned, release it all in one sudden, chaotic tumult like bats set free from the darkness of a cave.

The phone on Reardon's desk was ringing when he returned. He picked it up with one hand and pulled his chair under him with the other. "John Reardon."

"Mr. Reardon, this is Phillip Cardan. I understand you wanted to talk to me. I'm with Bailey, Merritt and White."

Reardon tried to picture the man who was speaking. Fortyish, paunchy, beset with nervous mannerisms; a slightly high-pitched voice, lacking the authority of a lawyer with significant courtroom experience; a man, Reardon suspected, who held a low-level position in the firm, advancing only in salary; perhaps, Reardon thought, though he could not be sure of this or anything else about Cardan at this point, a man on the make.

"That's right," Reardon replied cautiously, "I'm investigating the murder of Lee McDonald and her roommate."

"What's that got to do with me?" Cardan asked hurriedly.

"Well, I understand that——"

"She wasn't my secretary," Cardan interrupted.

"I didn't say she was," Reardon said.

"Well, I don't understand . . . I mean . . . Miss McDonald . . . I . . ."

"I understand that you had a more intimate relationship with Miss McDonald," Reardon said.

"Who told you that?" Cardan gasped. "I mean . . . I don't . . . I . . . I don't understand . . ."

"This is a murder investigation," Reardon said ominously.

"I didn't have anything to do with that," Cardan said.

Reardon said nothing, allowing his silence to sink into Cardan's mind like a heavy stone. He did not know what Cardan had to hide, but something between Cardan and Lee McDonald was whipping Cardan into a self-protecting frenzy. Maybe he had had an affair with her that the wife and kids in New Jersey would not be pleased to hear about. Maybe he was afraid Jamie O'Rourke would hear about it and flatten his head against a cement wall. Maybe he had killed Lee McDonald and Karen Ortovsky. Maybe anything.

"I didn't have anything to do with that," Cardan repeated, almost in a whisper. For another moment he said nothing, then he sighed resignedly. "She was supposed to be discreet," he said, with a touch of resentment.

"When did you see Lee McDonald last?" Reardon asked.

"Not over the phone," Cardan replied in a low, conspiratorial voice.

Reardon faked annoyance. "Where then?"

"The Sheep Meadow in Central Park," Cardan said.

"That's a big place."

"Meet me in the middle."

"That's a big place too," Reardon replied irritably.

"Carry a handkerchief in your hand."

"Forget it," Reardon snapped. "I'll see you in your office in fifteen minutes."

"No, no please!" Cardan pleaded. "Please don't. I have a reputation. I don't want to be seen in my office with the police, being questioned about murders. For God's sake."

Reardon said nothing.

"Please, do me this favor," Cardan said. "I'll take good care of you. Just please don't come over here. Meet me in the Sheep Meadow. In the middle."

"This is ridiculous," Reardon said.

"I'll make it worth your while," Cardan said.

"What time?"

"About a half hour from now."

"All right," Reardon agreed with feigned reluctance.

"Carry the white handkerchief," Cardan said. "Please."

"This better be worth it," Reardon said.

"Yes, yes, all right. One other thing," Cardan said, "come alone."

21

Standing in the middle of the Sheep Meadow, a white handkerchief dangling from his right hand, Reardon felt like a perfect ass. Surreptitious meetings in crowded locations were common enough, but the handkerchief gave the entire plan a character of silly melodrama. He wondered if this was the way it would all end for him, standing in some crowded public place, dangling a bandanna from his hand, waiting for a voice to materialize . . . and then, the flash of a gun, a shot, buckling knees and blackness.

A voice came from behind him. "Detective Reardon?"

Reardon turned to face a tall, heavy-set man dressed in a three-piece blue suit. He had a thin black mustache and tiny, reptilian eyes that made the elegantly tailored suit look like a costume.

Reardon nodded. "That's me."

"My name is Phillip Cardan."

"I wasn't expecting anyone else," Reardon said dryly.

Cardan thrust out his hand. "Thank you for coming," he said, as if he was welcoming Reardon to an art exhibition at some fashionable gallery.

Reardon did not take his hand.

For a moment Cardan stood with his hand outstretched and motionless like a department store manikin. Then he slowly withdrew it, placing it deep in his overcoat pocket. "Would you like to take a stroll?" he asked.

"I didn't come all the way out here for a stroll."

Cardan looked as though he had been physically assaulted. "Oh," he stammered. "I'm sorry."

"What's on your mind?" Reardon asked at once.

Cardan glanced nervously around the Sheep Meadow. "Let's walk and I'll tell you."

Reardon did not feel like arguing the point. Together they started walking slowly toward the west side of the park. A small wind crackled through the leafless trees on either side of the meadow. Reardon buried his hands in his overcoat pockets.

"Okay," he said, "what do you have to tell me?"

"Like you said," Cardan said, "Miss McDonald was indiscreet. She was supposed to be absolutely discreet. We had an agreement. She was to memorize everything. She was not to have anything in her apartment that could possibly connect her to me or to any of my associates."

"Like an address book?" offered Reardon.

"That's right," Cardan replied.

"I see," Reardon said, knowing he was getting close to something, suspecting that it was important, perhaps more important than he could have guessed.

Cardan offered Reardon a strained smile. "Before I go on," he said, "may I ask you a question?"

Reardon nodded.

"How did you come to associate me with Miss McDonald?"

"I can't tell you that," Reardon said crisply.

"I understand," Cardan said quickly, as if wishing he had not bothered to ask in the first place.

"Why did you want to know?" Reardon asked.

Cardan shrugged off the question. "It seemed odd, that's all."

Reardon did not believe that was all. "Why odd?" he asked. "You did have a relationship with Miss Mc-Donald, didn't you?"

"Yes," Cardan said. He looked up from the ground, nervously cast his eyes over the line of trees at the far side of the park, then let them fall directly on Reardon. "She was very unhappy with her life."

"I know that," Reardon barked belligerently, purposely pushing Cardan further.

Cardan flinched at Reardon's manner. "Can this be considered a voluntary statement, even if you already know everything I tell you?"

"If you're completely frank," Reardon said.

Cardan shook his head worriedly. "I don't know where to begin," he said. "I just want it all to be in confidence, that's all."

Reardon nodded. "We'll see."

Cardan stopped and looked helplessly at the ground. When he looked up again his face was flushed.

Reardon stared bloodlessly into Cardan's face and said nothing.

"You see," Cardan said, "Lee didn't like it in New York. She wanted desperately to get out of the States. To go to Europe. She and her roommate were planning on moving to France, I think. Anyway she needed money. And she couldn't get it. She couldn't save any money on her salary. So she came to me. She thought I might know of some way that she could get some extra money, savings, you know, for the move to Europe. So I helped her." He paused. "I need to be protected."

"From what?" Reardon asked.

"From being dragged into this case. Quite frankly,.

I didn't come forward before because I dreaded such a possibility. My reputation could be endangered if that connection were made public."

"Keep talking," Reardon said without emphasis.

"You see," Cardan said slowly, lowering his voice, "I did know the young women in question." He paused. "Rather well, actually." He looked at Reardon but said nothing.

"How well?" Reardon asked.

"You might say that I employed them from time to time."

"Employed them how?"

"That is the delicate point. You see, some friends of mine and I have a circle, you might say."

"What kind of circle?"

"An entertainment circle."

"You want to explain that?" Reardon asked coldly.

"It's not material."

Reardon stopped walking. "I'll decide what's material. You just answer the questions. You're the one who called me out here to the goddamn Sheep Meadow, remember?"

Cardan looked shaken, as if he was being shot at by a high-caliber pistol at point-blank range. "Sorry," he said meekly. "Of course I did. But I had hoped that all the details might not be necessary."

"This is a murder investigation," Reardon said bluntly. "That means that every detail is material."

Beads of sweat began to form on Cardan's upper lip, just above the little mustache. His hands fidgeted in his coat pockets. "Well," he said, "what I want to prove to you is simply that I could not have murdered those two women. My name could come up in the investigation and I simply need someone in the Department, the Police Department, to be aware of the fact that I could not possibly have been involved."

"In what way did you employ Karen Ortrovsky and Lee McDonald?" Reardon asked.

"In an unusual capacity."

"How?"

"Are you aware that Miss Ortovsky and Miss McDonald were lesbians?"

"Yes," Reardon said. He did not see how that mattered one way or the other.

"They also had another trait," Cardan said, "which turned out to be a profitable one for them."

"What?"

"Exhibitionism."

Reardon nodded.

"Some people are exhibitionists and some people are voyeurs," Cardan said.

"What's the point?" Reardon asked. He could guess that it was going to get pretty squalid now, and he wanted to get through it as quickly as possible. Such testimony always made him feel as if he was leaning over window sills into darkened bedrooms.

"Well," Cardan said, "some people in this city like to enjoy the . . . well, you might call them . . . you might call them *performances*. They enjoy seeing various sexual acts performed in front of them." Cardan smiled what Reardon took to be an ugly, leering smile.

"What does that have to do with murder?" Reardon asked.

"I don't believe it has anything whatsoever to do with murder."

"Did Karen Ortovsky and Lee McDonald give sexual performances?"

"Yes. They were not prostitutes, you must understand. They performed only with each other."

"For money?"

Cardan smiled. "For a great deal of money."

Reardon said nothing, letting his silence draw Cardan on.

"The point is," Cardan continued hesitantly, "I sometimes acted as their agent."

"For whom?"

"For certain people who desired their services."

From the way he talked, Reardon thought, you might have taken Cardan for a jewelry clerk at Tiffany's. "Wealthy people?" Reardon asked.

"Very wealthy people," Cardan replied. "Not the usual porno crowd."

Reardon did not understand the distinction. "Go on," he said.

"Simply this," Cardan said. "It will not be hard for the police assigned to the case to associate me with Miss Ortovsky and Miss McDonald. I knew them very well. I know a lot of people very well. But I could not have had anything to do with their murder. I was very saddened by it, as a matter of fact. But I was in California when it happened."

"Who did you arrange these performances for?"

"That's confidential."

"This is a murder case," Reardon said. "Nothing is confidential."

"I can assure you personally that none of my clients could possibly have had anything to do with the murders."

"You arranged for Karen Ortovsky and Lee McDonald to perform sexually for money, is that right?"

"I have already said that," Cardan said.

"You're under arrest."

Cardan was thunderstruck. His eyes widened in frenzied disbelief. "What!"

"You have a right to remain silent," Reardon began.

"You can't do that," Cardan exclaimed, his whole body trembling.

"Who are your clients?"

"No! I can't tell you that!"

"You have a right to an attorney," Reardon began again, his voice growing louder.

Cardan's eyes filled with tears. "That will ruin me," he pleaded. "For God's sake, I'm an attorney."

"Who are your clients?" Reardon asked again.

"Please! Please!" Cardan sputtered.

Reardon stopped. "Who are your clients?" he asked menacingly.

Breathlessly Cardan replied, "No more than ten or twelve people, that's all."

"I want them all," Reardon said.

Cardan frantically pulled a notebook from his coat pocket and began scribbling down the names. When he had finished he tore out the page and handed it to Reardon. "Here," he said.

Reardon grabbed the paper from his hand and looked at it. "This had better be all of them."

"It is," Cardan assured him, unnecessarily straightening his tie.

"If I find out that you left anybody off this list, I'll break your ass," Reardon said. "I'll hang you out to dry, do you understand what I'm telling you?"

"No one is left off," Cardan said. "You have my word."

"You may be hearing from me again," Reardon said, "after each of these people has been contacted."

"Wait!" Cardan exclaimed. "You can't contact them!"

Reardon began to walk away.

Cardan grabbed Reardon's arm and forcefully pulled him around. "You have to keep this in confidence. You said this would be in confidence!"

Reardon grabbed Cardan by his collar and pulled his face close to his own. "Sue me!" he said angrily, and threw Cardan backward with such force that the man stumbled to the ground.

As Reardon walked back across the Sheep Meadow he looked at the list Phillip Cardan had given him. One name gaped before him like a bloody mouth: Wallace Van Allen.

"Wallace Van Allen? Are you crazy?" Mathesson said in a voice so loud that several people in the precinct house turned toward him.

Reardon waited for the people in the precinct house to return their attention to whatever they had been doing before Mathesson's outburst. Then he handed Mathesson the list Cardan had given him.

Mathesson took the list and stared at it expressionlessly for a moment. He seemed to be studying it. Finally he looked up from the paper and glanced quickly left and right to make sure that he and Reardon could not be overheard.

"So what?" he said. "There are nine or ten other names on this list."

"But it's a connection," Reardon said.

"Bullshit," Mathesson said. "It's just a coincidence. Nothing else. But we've got a solid case against that little Petrakis creep."

"What about the women?"

Mathesson laughed. "So Wallace Van Allen gets his jollies by watching a couple of broads eat each other out. So what? There're so many guys like that, they'd have to hold their convention in Yankee Stadium." He looked at the list in Reardon's hand. "Those fucking names don't mean a goddamn thing."

"Are you telling me you don't believe the women and the deer were killed by the same man?"

Mathesson shrugged. "How the hell do I know?"

Reardon could not believe what he was hearing. "What about the blows and the numbers, that roman numeral two and the other one, dos?"

Mathesson dismissed the connection. "Go ask a gypsy fortune teller," he said.

"They were killed by the same man," Reardon said, decisively.

"Maybe," Mathesson said.

"How did Petrakis get in the apartment of those two women?" Reardon asked. "What would they have to do with a guy like him?"

"You're wearing me out, John," Mathesson said. "What exactly are you trying to say?"

"Until now there were two connections between the deer killings and the murders," Reardon said. "The number of blows in each case, and the dos and roman numeral two thing. Now there's a third connection, and that's Wallace Van Allen."

"You're going after Van Allen, aren't you?" Mathesson said.

"I'm following leads."

"You're creating leads."

Reardon took the list from Mathesson's hand. Mathesson stared at the list sadly, as if it were a document of sadness, a death certificate for a brilliant career. "It's being noticed by more people than me," he said.

"What is?"

"The way you're going after Van Allen." Mathesson stared bluntly at Reardon as if defying him to deny it.

"What the hell are you talking about?"

"What did you say to Van Allen when you talked to him that time in his penthouse?"

"I asked some questions."

"What kind of questions?"

"Just questions," Reardon said. "Mostly he did the talking."

"Well, I don't know what you said but you got him real edgy."

"What do you mean?"

"That's why Piccolini figured he had the authority to knock you off this case without getting reprimanded from downtown. Because Van Allen had already complained about you in a way."

"What way?"

"Well, he asked the people downtown if you were having him followed."

"If I was having him followed?" Reardon asked incredulously.

"That's right. Right after you talked to him. That night after you talked to him."

Reardon thought for a moment. "I talked to him on Tuesday afternoon," he said.

"That's right," Mathesson said, "and he called up on Wednesday morning and asked if you were having him tailed like a common crook. He said he was sure somebody'd been following him on Tuesday night."

Tuesday night, Reardon thought. "Wasn't that the night the women in the Village were murdered?"

"That's right," Mathesson said. "That's a good way to identify it."

* * *

So Wallace Van Allen thought he was being followed, Reardon thought. Why?

He decided to question Lee's and Karen's neighbor, Mrs. Malloy, again. He found her at her apartment amid the same tangle of Ziegfeld memorabilia. He suspected she had lived amidst it most of her life, the only legacy of her dead mother.

Her eyes brightened when she saw him at the door. "Detective Reardon," she said. "I didn't expect to see you again. Come in."

She opened the door widely. "Have a seat. Can I offer you a toddy?"

"No, thanks," Reardon said. He removed a pile of old movie magazines and sat down in a chair opposite Mrs. Malloy. "I just have a few questions for you," he said.

"Shoot."

Reardon took his notebook out of his pocket and reviewed it for a moment. "You said that you saw Miss Ortovsky and Miss McDonald about three A.M., is that right?"

"Yes," she said. "Sure you wouldn't like something? Anything? Coffee?"

"No, thank you. I just have a few things to straighten out. Probably doesn't mean anything. Just for my own curiosity, you might say."

"Well, all right," Mrs. Malloy said. "Suit yourself."

"When you saw the three people going up to the women's apartment that night," Reardon said, "did you see anybody following them?"

Mrs. Malloy thought a moment. "Well, I don't think so," she said finally.

"Are you sure?"

"Yes. Yes, I'm sure."

"You said you left your apartment not long after

they all went upstairs. On your way out of the building, did you see anyone who looked like he might be following them, or coming up to their apartment?"

Mrs. Malloy thought for a moment. "Well, at about eleven o'clock I heard someone knock at their door. There was a knock, some voices, then one of the women spoke to the man for a while, then the man went inside the apartment."

"Do you know when he left?" Reardon asked.

"Not exactly," Mrs. Malloy said, "but he couldn't have stayed for too long."

"Why not?"

"Because it wasn't but just a few minutes after he went in that them girls was at each other again."

Reardon nodded.

"He must have left before that," Mrs. Malloy said.

Reardon nodded and continued writing in his notebook.

Mrs. Malloy laughed. "Them two was moaning and groaning and screeching the bed springs to beat the band," she said.

What Reardon wanted to know was who was watching them.

22

Reardon had hardly sat down at his desk when Piccolini burst out of his office.

"There's another witness," Piccolini said. He stood directly in front of Reardon's desk, the noise and movement of the precinct house circling him like a whirlwind.

Reardon looked up. "Who?"

"Some old lady," Piccolini said. "She telephoned and the canvass went over to her home to ask some questions."

It was clear to Reardon that Piccolini was excited by the prospect of an eyewitness. Piccolini was really losing his reason over this case, Reardon thought. Anyone could say they were a witness to anything, but were they? And if so, what had they seen? And how well had they seen it? Nobody really had a witness until they had sufficient answers to those questions. He wondered why Piccolini had forgotten that. "What did she see?" he asked.

"She saw the man who killed the fallow deer."

"She's sure?"

"Yes," Piccolini said, smiling broadly.

"Did she describe him?" Reardon asked.

"I didn't go into that, but if it's Petrakis she saw, then that's it. No more nonsense. That's a conviction. Anyway, get over there." He handed Reardon a piece

215

of paper on which he had written the name and address of the witness:

Mrs. Eleanor Lassiter
203 East 69th Street

"Take a picture of Petrakis with you. She may be able to make a tentative identification from the photo."

"All right," Reardon said. He rose and began to put on his overcoat.

Piccolini rubbed his hands together eagerly. "The folks downtown are going to be real happy about this."

"Did you tell Van Allen yet?"

"Not yet," Piccolini replied. "Why?"

"Hold off a while."

Piccolini smiled, "Okay, I'll do that."

"Good," Reardon said.

"Just don't forget to take a picture of Petrakis. And call me the second she makes the identification. I want to know right away."

Reardon was getting a little weary of being instructed like a rookie. "All right," he said.

"This will tie it up," Piccolini said jubilantly. "I can just feel it. We got this case in the bag."

As he turned to walk back to his office Piccolini slapped Reardon affectionately on the back, as if they were old buddies again, fellow travelers on Saint Crispin's day: We few, we happy few, we band of brothers.

Reardon took a picture of Andros Petrakis and slipped it in one of his coat pockets. He suspected that Piccolini was right, that within the next few minutes Petrakis would either be convicted or cleared. Before now he had hoped for another witness as the only means of exonerating Petrakis. But now he had his doubts: the witness might identify Petrakis.

He stopped at a sidewalk newsstand to get a paper and was surprised to find that the *Daily News* was still carrying the killing of the fallow deer as its lead story. He turned to page two and was confronted once again with the faces of the three Van Allens and Andros Petrakis. He folded the paper back and read the story as he walked. There was nothing new. The killing was reiterated in one column. In another the activities of the Van Allen family in New York were traced through the previous fifty years. Another story related how the killing of the fallow deer had been held back by the press until a "suspect" was apprehended. Reardon tucked the newspaper under his arm. By this time tomorrow, he thought, he would be reading the story of the woman who saw the fallow deer slaughtered.

The closer he came to Mrs. Lassiter's address, the slower he walked. He did not want to interview her, and he knew it. If she identified Petrakis, then Reardon knew he had discredited himself, that he had trusted a feeling and the feeling had betrayed him. More importantly, it would mean that Petrakis had no hope of clearing himself, and even now Reardon could not believe that that insensible shadow of a man could possibly have roused himself to the brutal frenzy which the killing of the fallow deer required.

But if she could not identify Petrakis it would only mean that the case must be continued, and it had already exhausted Reardon like a fever. He knew that he had burned himself out on this case, lost the spirit of pursuit, the perverse energy of the chase itself. He had never had enough of that hunting instinct. But now even that animal vitality—the glint in the eye of the bird of prey—had fled him. He had no more questions left for Cain.

203 East 69th Street was a brownstone. It was clear to Reardon immediately that whoever the witness was she was a person of considerable means. It did not surprise him that a servant greeted him at the door.

"May I help you?" the woman asked. She was a small black woman dressed in a nurse's white uniform. She had a slight Jamaican accent.

"I'm Detective John Reardon, New York City Police Department." Reardon displayed his gold shield.

"I believe Mrs. Lassiter is expecting you. Won't you come in?" The woman opened the door and stepped back to let Reardon enter. "Would you mind waiting a moment?" she asked, and disappeared through a hallway adorned on both sides with paintings.

Looking around him Reardon realized that he had never seen a home so beautiful. Even the Van Allen penthouse lacked this subdued elegance. It was stately, even reverent. Everything—every book, piece of furniture and glass inlay—looked as though it had been carefully wrought by hands trained in a more patient age.

"Mr. Reardon?" a voice said.

Reardon felt as though he had been wrenched from a brief reverie. He turned around in the direction of the voice. "Yes?"

"Mrs. Lassiter is in her garden," the black woman said. "She would prefer meeting you there."

"That would be fine," Reardon said.

She conducted Reardon through the hall of paintings and out into a small, shaded Japanese rock garden surrounding a shallow, irregular pool. Water trickled through a bamboo pipe, over a large stone and into the pool.

"This is Detective Reardon," the woman said to Mrs. Lassiter.

"Won't you sit down?" Mrs. Lassiter asked.

"Yes, thank you," Reardon said. He sat down in a small rattan chair. "This is a lovely garden."

"It's pleasant," Mrs. Lassiter replied, "but it is not Heaven." She was bundled up in a heavy blue coat which, complemented the grayness of her eyes. Her head was covered by a thick wool shawl and her hands were tightly clothed in brown suede gloves. She sat in a large white wicker chair near the center of the garden. She was very old, or so she appeared to Reardon. The hair that crept out from underneath the shawl was white. Still, her face retained a beauty that Reardon guessed had once been extraordinary.

"You are here about the deer, I suppose?" she said.

Reardon laid the newspaper on a table that stood between himself and Mrs. Lassiter and took out his notebook. "I understand that you have some information which might help us."

"Yes," Mrs. Lassiter said, "I have."

Reardon nodded for her to proceed, but she did not. Instead she said, "I'm sorry that I could not receive you inside."

"That's all right," Reardon said.

"It is difficult for me to move," Mrs. Lassiter explained. She glanced at her gloved hands. "I have very severe arthritis. There are times when any movement is extremely painful for me."

"I'm sorry," Reardon said.

"I don't like to receive guests in the garden," Mrs. Lassiter continued. "It never seemed to me to be a proper place." She smiled. "Especially so late in the fall."

"I wouldn't worry about it," Reardon said.

"Perhaps not," Mrs. Lassiter said. "Things are much more casual now than when I was a girl. Things were very formal then, you know. Such formality is thought to be rigid now. My grandchildren, for example, are most informal in everything."

"I see," Reardon said, letting her go on, work herself up to what she had seen—if, in fact, she had really seen anything.

"Most informal," Mrs. Lassiter repeated. She paused. "Are you married?"

"I was married," Reardon said.

Mrs. Lassiter lowered her eyes. "Oh, divorced," she said quietly.

"No," Reardon explained, "my wife died."

"Oh," Mrs. Lassiter said, "I'm sorry."

"It's quite all right," Reardon said.

"Divorce is very prevalent now," Mrs. Lassiter said, looking somewhat apologetic.

"Yes, it is."

"A shame, I think," Mrs. Lassiter said, "families breaking up like that. Sacred covenants broken." She paused to watch a small breeze skirt a flank of dead leaves across the garden. "Were you married only once?"

"Yes."

Mrs. Lassiter nodded approvingly. "Any children?"

"One," Reardon said, "one son."

"I see," Mrs. Lassiter said. "I have two daughters. They——"

"Mrs. Lassiter?" Reardon interrupted. It was time, now, to move on.

"They have both been married," Mrs. Lassiter continued, undeterred. "Now they're both divorced. I suppose that's the way things are now."

Reardon was beginning to wonder if Mrs. Lassiter had seen anything at all. He remembered all the times before when lonely people had called the police with no more justification than a desire to talk to someone —anyone—about anything. The falsely reported burglaries, noises, assaults outside their doors, faces reflected in late-night windowpanes. Reardon suspected that Mrs. Lassiter might identify anyone, any photo that he showed her.

"Mrs. Lassiter," Reardon began again, "about the deer . . ."

"Oh, yes," Mrs. Lassiter said. "Of course, that's why you're here. Forgive me for my digression." She smiled faintly. "It is said to be a prerogative of old age."

"One of our officers reported that you had information that might be of help to us."

"Yes," Mrs. Lassiter said, "I have." Her voice was full of authority, and Reardon could not doubt that she, herself, did at least believe that her information was important.

"Can you tell me?" he asked politely.

"Of course," Mrs. Lassiter said. Painfully, she shifted a bit in her seat. "I was in the park when the deer were killed."

Reardon jotted down her first statement in his notebook. "I see." He looked up at Mrs. Lassiter. "About what time was that?"

"I'm not sure."

"You're not?" Perhaps she had not seen anything at all, he thought, if she did not know the time of the crime.

"It was sometime in the early morning."

"I see," Reardon said. "Which morning?"

"Monday morning, a week ago Monday morning."

Reardon noted her response down in his notebook. Everything she had said so far, he thought, had been in the newspapers. "Do you have any idea when on Monday morning you were in the Children's Zoo?" Point by point he expected the credibility of her story to disintegrate. "Had the sun come up, do you remember? Was it after dawn?"

"No," she replied firmly. "It was not. It was still very dark. I am sure of that."

"I see," Reardon said.

"It was very dark," Mrs. Lassiter repeated, "except, of course, for the lights that illuminate the zoo at night."

"Of course," Reardon said, looking up. "So you were in the Children's Zoo early Monday morning, before daylight. Were you alone?"

"Yes."

"You were alone in the Children's Zoo at that hour?" Reardon asked again, and it was clear that he doubted it.

"Yes," Mrs. Lassiter said authoritatively, "I was."

"Why?"

Mrs. Lassiter did not answer.

"It's kind of unusual," Reardon said, "for anyone to be in the park at that hour."

"Yes," Mrs. Lassiter said, looking away, "I suppose it is."

"Could you tell me why you were there?"

"That is very personal," Mrs. Lassiter said.

"If it has no bearing on the case," Reardon assured her, "then anything you say is confidential. I promise you."

Mrs. Lassiter bowed her head. "I don't know if I can," she said.

Reardon leaned toward her. "Mrs. Lassiter, I have been a policeman in New York for about thirty years."

Mrs. Lassiter looked up and smiled. "I suppose you have heard or seen every possible wickedness?"

"Yes, I think so," Reardon said.

Mrs. Lassiter's face relaxed, but her lower lip began to tremble. "Have you ever been in great pain?" she asked.

"Physical pain?" Reardon asked. "No. No, I haven't."

"Look at my hands," Mrs. Lassiter said.

Reardon looked down at Mrs. Lassiter's hands. They were curled delicately around the arms of her chair. He could guess what they looked like under the gloves.

"I cannot straighten my fingers," she said. "There are days when I cannot move at all because the pain is too great. There are days when I cannot raise a fork to my lips to feed myself, and so I have to be fed and my mouth has to be wiped like an infant."

"I see," Reardon said. He could feel a tension building in his own hands, tightening his fingers.

"Do you?" Mrs. Lassiter asked. "I don't think you do."

"It's your arthritis?" Reardon asked.

"Yes," Mrs. Lassiter said, and she stared at him with a face as full of rage at the awesome humiliation of her distress as Reardon had ever seen. "There are times when I can do no more for myself than the tiniest infant. Times when I cannot clean myself."

Reardon leaned back in his chair and tried to relax the rage he felt might rise in him at any moment. He wanted to lift her up, fold her in gossamer, and send her to the place where earthbound things have wings. But he could not even speak.

Mrs. Lassiter was silent for a moment. She sat, lips

trembling, trying to compose herself. "But that does not really tell you what I was doing in the Children's Zoo before dawn on a Monday morning," she said finally.

"No," Reardon admitted, "it doesn't."

"I don't want to live like this," Mrs. Lassiter said.

Reardon nodded. He felt helpless, unable to do anything else.

"Are you a Catholic, Detective Reardon?" she asked.

"In a way."

"An apostate?"

"In a way," Reardon said again.

"But you are enough of a Catholic to know that in our faith suicide is a mortal sin?"

"Yes."

"All my life," Mrs. Lassiter said, "I have been a devout Catholic."

Reardon nodded.

"A practicing Catholic," Mrs. Lassiter added.

"Yes," Reardon said.

For a moment Mrs. Lassiter could not speak.

Reardon waited, then he urged her on. "A practicing Catholic," he said.

"Yes," Mrs. Lassiter said, "a devout and practicing Catholic who cannot bear to live anymore."

"I see," Reardon said.

"Have you ever heard the story of David and Uriah?" Mrs. Lassiter said.

"No."

"King David in the Bible? And Uriah?"

"No."

"Well, Uriah was a soldier in the army of Israel. He had a beautiful wife, and David wanted her for himself. But David did not believe in adultery. And he did not believe in outright murder. So he sent Uriah to the most deadly position in a battle, and Uriah was killed there."

Mrs. Lassiter looked at Reardon. "Do you know what I mean?"

"I'm not sure," Reardon said.

"I am David," Mrs. Lassiter said.

"David?"

"*And* Uriah," she added.

Then Reardon understood why Mrs. Lassiter had been in the Children's Zoo so early on a Monday morning. But he did not know what he could say or do in response to that knowledge. Quickly he leaned forward and picked a dead leaf from Mrs. Lassiter's lap and dropped it soundlessly into the pool beside her.

"I want to die but I cannot kill myself," Mrs. Lassiter said, "so I go to dangerous secluded places."

It seemed to Reardon that a wave of relief passed over her with that final, direct admission. "Like the Children's Zoo?" he asked.

"Yes."

"I'm sorry."

"Thank you," Mrs. Lassiter said.

Reardon noted how quickly she had regained her composure. It was obvious to him that she neither needed nor wanted pity; what she wanted was to die, to be done with it. In the meantime she would carry on as best she could.

"You may continue your questions, Detective Reardon," she said.

"Why don't you just tell me what you saw?" Reardon said, exhausted.

Mrs. Lassiter nodded politely. "I was walking down the sidewalk which runs near the elephant cages and into the plaza behind the main building, the one at the

Fifth Avenue entrance to the zoo. I had been walking all about the park that evening. I had not seen many people. As I said, I am not sure of the time."

"Yes, go on."

"Well, as I reached the southern corner of the main building, I saw a man running toward me with an ax in his hand. He was covered with blood. He was looking behind him as he ran, and it was not until he was almost on me, not more than a few feet away, that he turned forward and saw me."

"And you saw him?" Reardon asked.

"Very clearly," Mrs. Lassiter said, "and I have never seen a face so full of fear. I thought for a moment that he must have been attacked himself. The way he looked so frightened, the way he was running, looking behind him."

"What did he do when he saw you?"

"He stopped. And he just looked at me," Mrs. Lassiter said. "I thought he was going to collapse at my feet and beg me to protect him. He was weeping, you see. Crying so hard that his whole body was shaking."

"Crying?"

"Oh, yes," Mrs. Lassiter said, "very definitely. I have no doubt of that. He was crying, almost convulsively. We were standing on the sidewalk. It was well lit, and I saw him as plainly as I could see you in this garden if you were a few feet distant. Then he turned and ran in the other direction."

"Which direction?"

"He ran directly north, away from me. Then he turned and disappeared behind the main building. Toward the stairs that exit the park onto Fifth Avenue."

Reardon jotted this down in his notebook. "What did he do with the ax?"

"He took it with him."

"You're sure he didn't drop it or throw it away?"

"No," Mrs. Lassiter said, "he took it with him. He still had it when he ran out of sight."

"I see," Reardon said. He took a photograph of Andros Petrakis from his coat pocket and handed it to Mrs. Lassiter. "Is this the man you saw?"

Mrs. Lassiter took the photograph and examined it. Then she looked up at Reardon and smiled. "You detectives are so curious," she said.

Reardon was puzzled. "What do you mean?"

"This photo. I suppose you have to do these things."

"What things?"

"Tests, I suppose you would call them. I mean the way you give me a photograph of a man I have never seen before in my life and leave a picture of the real man sitting right in front of me."

"What?"

"The newspaper," Mrs. Lassiter said.

Reardon glanced down at the newspaper and the three pictures of the Van Allen family. "One of them?" he asked.

"Why, yes," Mrs. Lassiter replied, puzzled by Reardon's apparent surprise.

"Which one?" Reardon asked quietly.

Laboriously Mrs. Lassiter raised her arm and pointed toward the faces staring back at her from the newspaper. "Him," she said.

"Wallace Van Allen?"

"The second one down."

Reardon put his index finger on the face of Dwight Van Allen. "Him?"

"Yes," Mrs. Lassiter said.

"Are you sure?"

"Yes."

"You can make a positive identification?"

"Yes."

"Of this man?" Reardon thumped the picture of Dwight Van Allen with his finger.

"Yes," Mrs. Lassiter said. "I recognized the face even before I read about the deer."

Reardon was not at all sure he believed her. She had told him nothing she could not have taken from the papers. For a moment he was furious at Piccolini for releasing the critical information that the murder weapon was an ax.

"But you don't know exactly when you were in the Children's Zoo," he said.

"Not exactly," Mrs. Lassiter said. "Only that it was before dawn."

"And what did you say he had in his hand when he ran toward you?"

"An ax."

"Do you remember what it looked like? Was it large? Or was it small? Could it have been a hatchet?"

"No," Mrs. Lassiter said decisively, "it was an ax about three or four feet long."

Reardon nodded. "And you didn't see what he did with it?"

"When he ran out of my sight he still had it."

Quickly Reardon's mind raced over the things she had said. He wondered about everything, questioned everything: her vision; her memory; her arthritis; her desire for death; even whether or not she had actually been in the Children's Zoo that night. "Are you willing to testify in court as to what you saw?" he asked, knowing she would say yes.

"I would not have come forward if I had not been willing to testify in court," she said.

"Why did you wait so long to talk to the police?" Reardon asked, knowing it would be one of the firs questions Dwight Van Allen's defense attorney would ask her on the stand.

"I wasn't sure a crime had been committed," Mrs. Lassiter said. "At first I checked the papers every day after that Monday morning, but there was nothing there, so what was there to report? Then I went away for a few days. When I came back, I saw the paper. I called the police and one of your officers came to my house, so I told him what I had seen."

Reardon nodded. "Dwight Van Allen," he said almost to himself. He stood up. "Thank you for coming forward."

"I'll escort you to the door," Mrs. Lassiter said.

"That won't be necessary," Reardon said.

"No, no," Mrs. Lassiter insisted. "I still make feeble attempts at good manners."

Reardon smiled.

"Excuse me a moment," Mrs. Lassiter said.

Reardon watched as Mrs. Lassiter painfully stood and reached behind her chair. She brought out her walker and used it to balance herself. Her eyes returned to Reardon.

"I am unable to walk without assistance," she explained. "Now, may I show you out?"

"Fine, thank you," Reardon said, and together they took the first step toward the door.

It was then that Reardon heard it: a sound at once muffled and grating on the flagstone walk of the garden. It was the same sound, Reardon realized instantly, that Noble had heard the night the fallow deer were killed. Immediately Reardon stepped in front of Mrs. Lassiter and stared down at the four legs of the walker. Three of them were sheathed with rubber tips; they had made the muffled sound as she placed the walker in front of her. But one of the tips was bare and made a sound of metal dragging across stone.

An icy wave of recognition passed over Reardon's body. "Did you use this walker in the Children's Zoo the night the deer were killed?" he asked.

Mrs. Lassiter stared at him with confusion. "Of course," she said. "I cannot walk without it."

Reardon took a deep breath and exhaled slowly, staring almost transfixed at the walker.

23

For a long time after talking to Mrs. Lassiter, Reardon
sat in the park thinking, his mind filled with images:
weapons, distances, sounds, directions, motives, crumpled bodies. Images on top of images, thoughts con-
suming thoughts, until there was nothing left but a
mood, an atmosphere at once indistinct and profound:
sadness and resolution combined with an intense desire
for release from the park, the street, the city, from the
face of Karen Ortovsky, the futile bleating of the fallow
deer, the whirr of the ax blade slicing through the air.
He wanted to be something else besides a detective, a
widower, a man.

He had expected to be pleased if Mrs. Lassiter
cleared Petrakis. And there was no doubt in his mind
that Mrs. Lassiter's statement had cleared Petrakis entirely. But the cowering, weeping figure she had described as the real killer seemed to Reardon to be no
less pitiable than Petrakis. Now he would have to go
after Dwight Van Allen like a trained hunting dog,
switching indifferently from one fox to another.

When he returned to the precinct house Reardon
walked directly to Piccolini's office. He did not have
any time to waste. Petrakis' mood seemed too unpre-

dictable, and Reardon wanted to get him out of the Tombs as quickly as possible.

Piccolini looked up from a roast beef sandwich as Reardon entered the office. "Well, what did she say?" he asked. In one long burst Reardon told him, repeating his exchange with Mrs. Lassiter almost word for word. He described the way she looked, the way she spoke, why she had been in the park at such an unusual hour, and the sounds the walker made as it scraped across the garden pavement. With each new detail Piccolini's mouth seemed to open wider. He pushed the sandwich to the left side of his desk and stared intently at Reardon.

Finally Reardon reached the critical element in the interrogation. "She identified Dwight Van Allen as the man with the ax," he said.

Piccolini bolted back in his chair as if he had been slugged in the chest. "Dwight Van Allen?"

"That's who she identified."

Piccolini stood up. "Dwight Van Allen? Are you crazy?"

"She made a positive identification."

The technical term "positive identification" seemed to impress Piccolini for a moment. He sat back down behind his desk and stared inconsolably at the papers which littered it. "But that's crazy," he said. He pounded his fist hard on the desk. "Goddamn this fucking case!"

Reardon was startled by Piccolini's sudden use of obscenity; he usually avoided such language. Reardon had always suspected that he did so in order to prove some imagined superiority.

"Anyway," Reardon said, "Petrakis is clear."

"Why's that?"

It seemed simple to Reardon. "Because the only living witness in the case identified another man, Dwight Van Allen."

"An old woman with a crazy story about looking to be murdered in the park?" Piccolini said contemptuously. "You call that a witness?"

"She was there," Reardon said emphatically. "The sounds that walker made fit the sounds that Noble heard around the time the deer were killed."

"Ridiculous," Piccolini said, "I don't think she saw anything. I think she's a lonely old broad with a vivid imagination. Unfortunately, Dwight Van Allen got stuck in her mind somewhere."

"She saw him," Reardon said. "She saw him covered with blood and carrying an ax."

"What does the great detective, John Reardon, think was the motive for Dwight Van Allen to kill those deer?"

"I don't know," Reardon said, "but I'm going to find out."

Piccolini jumped to his feet. "No!" he shouted. "The people downtown are sick and tired of you meddling with the Van Allens."

"Dwight Van Allen is a prime suspect in this case," Reardon said.

Piccolini strode angrily around his desk to face Reardon. "Petrakis had a motive and he was seen near the scene of the crime at approximately the time of its commission," he said. "He had access to the murder weapon, and his fingerprints are all over it. That's real evidence, not some idiotic hallucination by some lonely old lady who's probably crazy as hell anyway."

Reardon turned to leave; he had heard enough.

"That's evidence," Piccolini repeated. "Build a case on that. Real evidence. Physical evidence."

Reardon stopped in the doorway, his hand on the doorknob. "Be careful, Mario," he said.

"About what?"

"About this case. About who did it. About avoiding a frame-up."

Piccolini's face quickly went through phases of anger, then shock, then sadness. "Is that what you think I'm trying to do in this case, John? Do you think I'm trying to frame Petrakis?"

"Sometimes it just happens."

"I wouldn't do that," Piccolini said.

Reardon looked at Piccolini and saw that he really believed himself incapable of such a thing. It was as if he was a little like Benedict Arturo, unconscious of his urges and even of the acts that flowed from them. For a moment Reardon thought of going over the entire case with Piccolini, demonstrating how each of his decisions had moved the investigation toward Petrakis. But he did not. It would only be a series of futile allegations which Piccolini would deny. Piccolini would not even have to lie to deny them, at least not to himself. Reardon did not want to talk to Piccolini anymore or be in his office ever again. "I think I'm going to retire after this one, Mario," he said.

Piccolini stared rigidly at Reardon. He would not, Reardon knew, try to dissuade him from early retirement, not after this.

Reardon had a witness, but he did not have a motive. And there was only one place where he could find one. He left the precinct house immediately and headed toward the Van Allen residence on Fifth Avenue. His old colleague, Steadman, was again on duty at the door.

"Is Wallace Van Allen in?" Reardon asked.

"No," Steadman said. "He's in Washington."

"How about Dwight?"

"He's gone to school in Massachusetts." Steadman looked at Reardon curiously. "You look beat."

"Is Melinda Van Allen in Massachusetts too?" Reardon asked dryly.

"No, she's in the park. In the zoo I guess."

"Thanks," Reardon said. He turned to leave.

Steadman grabbed his arm. "Is she expecting you?"

Reardon pulled his arm from Steadman's grasp. "Do you have a buzzer system in the park?" he asked irritably, and immediately felt ashamed.

"No," Steadman said, but he smiled, almost gently, as if something told him to be kind, and Reardon felt relieved.

"Melinda's in the zoo, you think?" he said.

"Yeah."

"Well, I'll see if I can find her."

Melinda Van Allen was not hard to find. She was sitting on the same bench where Reardon had talked to her before, just beyond the cage of the fallow deer. She had drawn the collar of her coat up around her neck to protect her from the light breezes that darted through the park.

She looked up from a book as Reardon approached. "Hello," she said brightly.

"Hello, Miss Van Allen," Reardon said. "I'd like to talk to you if it's okay."

"Sure," Melinda replied airily. "It's John, isn't it?"

"Yes, that's right."

"Detective John Reardon, New York City Police Department," she said in a deep voice with mock seriousness.

"May I sit down?"

"The park is for the people," Melinda said.

Sometimes, Reardon thought as he sat down, the park is for killing.

"Is this business or pleasure?" Melinda asked pleasantly. She put her book facedown on the bench beside her and folded her arms in front of her, pressing her bare hands under them for warmth.

"Business," Reardon said.

Melinda's face darkened.

"Who lives in your apartment?" Reardon asked.

"My father, my brother and myself," Melinda said. Then she added: "And a few servants."

"Do all of you usually live together?"

"We have until now."

"What do you mean?"

"Well, Dwight's gone off to school."

"When did he leave?"

"Yesterday," Melinda said. "I'll be leaving next week myself."

"Same school as your brother?"

"No," Melinda said, "but nearby."

"Are you two very close?" Reardon asked hesitantly.

"Yes. Very. We're twins, you know." She seemed proud of that fact.

"Yes, I know."

Melinda smiled. "We're duplicates, practically," she said enthusiastically. "When we were younger and we had to sign something, you know jointly, like a wedding or Christmas card from both of us, we wouldn't sign our names separately."

"You wouldn't?"

"No," Melinda said, "we'd just sign with the number 'two.' "

Reardon had not expected anything like this so quickly. "With a digit?" he asked.

"Sometimes," Melinda said, "or sometimes with the number written out, sometimes in a foreign language."

"Or a roman numeral?"

"Sure," Melinda said. "That was Dwight's favorite."

Reardon peered over Melinda's shoulder to the empty cage of the fallow deer. The long thin shadows from the bars fell slantwise across its floor. The chalk marks were beginning to fade. "When did your father give you the deer?"

"Three years ago. It was our birthday."

"And not quite two years ago he donated them to the Children's Zoo in your name."

"In both our names." Melinda looked at Reardon quizzically. "Why all these questions?"

"You and Dwight are very close, you say?" Reardon asked. He was stalling, and he knew it.

"Yes," Melinda said, "very close."

Reardon nodded. He was not sure what to do next. He was not sure that Melinda was prepared to go to the place he knew he had to take her.

"What is this all about?" she asked again. "Reardon, the mysterious detective." Jokingly she deepened her voice. "Does the Shadow know?"

"Do you know who killed the fallow deer?" Reardon asked bluntly.

Melinda grimaced. "No," she said emphatically, "I don't." She laughed, but she could not conceal her distress. "Do you know who killed them?" she asked tauntingly.

"We have a witness," Reardon said quietly. "We have a woman who saw the man who killed the deer."

"Well, who did it?" Melinda asked excitedly. "No more phony mystery. Who killed them?"

Reardon stood up. "Melinda, I want to show you something."

"Where?"

"Here," Reardon replied. "Here in the zoo. Just a little ways from here."

"All right," Melinda said. She stood up, putting her book away in her bag. "This better be worth it, though. It's hard to get a seat at this bench sometimes. I wouldn't give it up for just anyone, you know." She smiled at Reardon.

"It's just right over here," Reardon said. He pointed to the cage of the fallow deer.

Melinda stepped back. "No," she said. "I don't want to go over there."

Reardon took her arm gently. "It's just an empty cage now," he said. "It's important." He led her forward delicately. "Please."

"I can't," Melinda said. She took another step back.

Reardon still held her arm. "Please," he said emphatically, more like an order than a request.

"Oh, all right," Melinda said. "I'm a big girl now. Right?"

"Right," Reardon said.

Together they walked through the police barricades and into the cage of the fallow deer. The chalk outlines of the bodies had faded considerably, although they were still visible beneath patches of dried leaves and litter. A sudden gust of wind rattled the tin roof of the shed, and Reardon felt Melinda's arm tremble.

"I want you to look at something," he said.

Melinda's face was tense. "What?"

Reardon walked toward the rear of the cage, picked up a piece of tin about a foot square and, holding it facedown, brought it back to where Melinda stood.

"This is part of the deer shed," he said. "I asked for it to be brought back over here from the lab this morning."

"What lab?"

"The crime lab."

Melinda nodded fearfully. Standing within the black bars of the cage, her arms nestling her body, protecting it from the cold, she looked like an abandoned child, and Reardon wondered whether he could ever justify what he was about to do to her.

"This piece of the shed is evidence now," he said.

"What do you mean?"

"I want to show you something, Melinda," Reardon said tenderly. "It may not mean anything, but I think it does." He could see that her hand was beginning to tremble. "I think you'll know what it means," he said. He looked at her now as if he would never see another human face, as if Melinda Van Allen were the only person left on earth, and he, Reardon, was about to disclose a terrible thing to her that would poison her life forever.

Slowly he turned the square of tin around. Scrawled clearly on the other side, in dark red, was the roman numeral "two."

Melinda gasped.

"It's written in the blood of one of the deer," Reardon said.

"Oh, no," she said.

Reardon watched her. She did not look at him. She did not move. She only continued to stare at the square of tin.

"It doesn't really mean anything, does it?" she asked fearfully.

"Not by itself," Reardon admitted. "But we have a

witness. This witness saw a person running away from the deer cage. He was carrying an ax and he was covered with blood."

Again Reardon paused. Melinda stared at him silently, helplessly, and Reardon knew that he did not want to go on with it. But all of this commitment to the work he had chosen so long ago seemed suddenly to focus on the fact that he had to go on with it. That it was out of his hands now. That something more important than himself or Melinda or even Petrakis was demanding that he go on.

"She identified a picture of your brother Dwight as the man she saw with the ax," he said.

Melinda closed her eyes and drew a deep breath. She seemed to shrink into her clothes, to wither under Reardon's gaze.

"Where was Dwight the night the fallow deer were killed?" he asked.

Instantly her eyes shot open. "He was with me!" she blurted.

"No, he wasn't," Reardon said sadly. He took Melinda by the arm and, still carrying the piece of the deer shed, led her to a bench outside the cage. He put the piece of tin across his lap as they sat down. "Dwight wrote this, didn't he?" he asked.

"No," Melinda snapped. "He was with me that night."

"No, Melinda."

"Yes." She would not look at him now. She sat sullenly beside him and stared dreamily at her shoes, as if to look at him would be to admit that what he said was true.

"Until three in the morning?" he asked.

"Yes."

"What did you do that night?"

She did not answer.

"You spent the whole night together," Reardon said insistently. "What did you do?"

"We went to a movie."

"When did you go to the movie?"

"I'm not sure."

"What time did you get back?"

Melinda shifted uncomfortably on the bench and chewed on her lower lip like a resentful child.

"What time did you get back?" Reardon asked again.

"I'm not sure about that either."

"What movie did you see?"

"I don't remember."

"You don't remember what movie?"

"I can't think."

"Try."

"I can't! I told you I can't!"

"Well, you didn't spend the whole night in a movie," Reardon said, "so what did you do when you got back?"

"I don't know for sure. Maybe we played cards."

"All night?"

"Maybe we watched television."

"All night?"

"Maybe." She was beginning to whimper now, and Reardon did not know what to do about that. He stared at her helplessly, his palms faceup in his lap as if giving up on a riddle. He only knew that he must go on, that he must pursue her until he captured her brother.

"What card games did you play?" he asked.

She did not answer.

"So you went to a movie you can't remember the name of, you don't know when you went, and you don't know when you got back to the apartment, and you don't remember what you did when you got there. Is that what you're telling me?"

Melinda turned her face away from him and riveted her attention on some distant object in the park.

"How about Tuesday night and early Wednesday morning?" Reardon asked, fixing his mind on the only imperative he knew: to protect Abel against the rage of Cain.

Melinda looked at him. "What do you mean?"

"The Wednesday morning after the deer were killed. Where were you between three A.M. and eight A.M. that morning?"

"Why?"

"Where were you?"

"I want to know why you're asking."

"There's more involved than the deer."

Melinda stared at him fearfully. "What do you mean?"

"Two days after the deer were killed two women were murdered in Greenwich Village. The women were killed exactly like the deer, the same number of blows. One of the women was cut to pieces. The other just had her throat cut. Your father knew both those women."

"So what?" Melinda asked with attempted haughtiness.

"Melinda," he pleaded, "it's no good. The word 'dos' was written on the wall of one of their rooms."

He saw her pale in horror. She stared at him, wide-eyed, as if hoping to see something in his face that would deny what he'd said.

"It was written in their blood," he said.

Melinda lowered her head and began to cry gently.

"Dwight followed your father there. He waited until he left their apartment. Then Dwight killed two women not much older than yourself."

"Oh, God," Melinda whispered.

"What I have to know," Reardon said, "is why he did that. Why he killed the deer and the women."

Suddenly Melinda's face hardened. "It's *his* fault," she said bitterly.

"Whose?"

"His," she said, spitting out the word. "My father's. You don't know what it's like living with him."

"No, I don't," Reardon said.

Melinda stared out across the park. "He used to humiliate Dwight all the time. He used to call him stupid, say that Dwight wasn't his real son, that there'd been a mistake in the hospital, and my father's real son went to someone else, and he got Dwight." She turned to Reardon. "Have you ever met him?"

"Your father?"

"No, Dwight."

"I passed him in an elevator once."

"You passed him in an elevator?"

"Yes."

Melinda smiled bitterly. "What a strange job you have," she said.

Stranger than she knew, Reardon thought, stranger than mourning and the Buddha's solution to it, stranger than anything she would likely ever know.

"We made a party for my father the night the deer were killed," she said. "Dwight and I. For his birthday. For his fifty-seventh birthday. But he never showed up. I don't know how many times Dwight reminded him about the party that day. He kept reminding him all day. But he never showed up." Her eyes narrowed hatefully. "If it had been Dwight's birthday, he would have been there."

"Why?" Reardon asked.

"Because my father was a kind of closet sadist when it came to Dwight."

"What do you mean?"

"Oh, I don't mean a real sadist. It wasn't like he really beat Dwight." She sneered. "That would never be tolerated by his circle of friends. But there was a certain way he looked sometimes, a certain look in his eye. Do you know what I mean?"

"I guess," Reardon said. He had seen cruelty split its mask.

"And there was one place, one time when it really came out," she said. "On Dwight's birthday."

"His birthday?"

"Yes. On Dwight's birthday my father would bend him over his knee and start hitting him, you know, on his backside. Then he'd really beat him. And each time he'd hit Dwight, he'd call out a number. You know: One. Whack. Two. Whack. Three. Whack!" With each number, she struck the sheet of tin on Reardon's lap. "Last year it went to fifteen," she said, tears filling her eyes, her shoulders beginning to shake as she began to cry. She raised her hand and brought it down angrily on the tin. "Fourteen. Whack! Fifteen. Whack!" and her hand made the tin reverberate across the Children's Zoo. She was crying almost hysterically now. She raised her arm high above her head and brought her hand down furiously on the sheet of tin. "And one to grow on!" she shouted, and then collapsed in convulsive weeping. "Dwight said he'd like to give it back to my father someday," she said through her crying. "Fifty-seven. And one to grow on."

Fifty-seven and one, thought Reardon. Dear God.

He drew Melinda under his arm. She was sobbing uncontrollably now; he could feel her body convulsing against his own, her tears falling on his hand. "All right, all right," he said gently, knowing that it was not all right, that it never could be.

24

Reardon went directly to Piccolini's office after his encounter with Melinda Van Allen. He did not feel victorious or jubilant, and he related the details of his conversation with Melinda in a weary, unemphatic voice. Piccolini's eyes remained riveted on Reardon throughout his report. He shook his head dejectedly from time to time, but Reardon was unable to fathom exactly what that meant.

"What are your conclusions?" Piccolini asked after Reardon had finished.

Reardon did not hesitate. "Dwight Van Allen should be arrested on suspicion of murder immediately. I don't think we have any time to waste."

"Well, I don't know," Piccolini said. He stood up and thrust out his hand. "But you've done a great job, John. I mean it. It was a hassle, but you did fine work."

Reardon took Piccolini's hand but said nothing. He could not understand why Piccolini was balking on the arrest.

"I don't know if we can act right away with the arrest of the Van Allen boy," Piccolini explained peremptorily as he resumed his seat behind his desk, "but I think we may have the beginning of a case."

"The beginning of a case?" Reardon asked, astonished. "Are you saying you're not going to arrest Dwight Van Allen just as quick as you find him?"

"Yes," Piccolini said without hesitation. "That's exactly what I'm saying." He waved his hand as if dismissing Reardon from his office and began to fumble through some papers on his desk as if he were looking for something.

"Why not?" Reardon demanded.

Piccolini looked up. He seemed almost surprised to see Reardon still in his office. "Well, the evidence is still somewhat soft," he said. "The old lady's testimony is kinky, you know, her being such an eccentric and all. I mean, that stuff about trying to get somebody to kill her. Don't you know what a defense attorney would do with that?" Piccolini casually returned his attention to the papers on his desk. "And the rest of the case is pretty circumstantial," he added offhandedly.

Reardon leaned forward, pressing his palms on Piccolini's desk. "Two women are dead. Let the DA worry about a soft case. I want Dwight Van Allen off the streets."

"I know two women are dead," Piccolini said defensively.

"Arrest Van Allen," Reardon repeated.

"I can't," Piccolini said.

"Why not?"

"Because he's not on the streets anymore."

"He's in Massachusetts at some college," Reardon said.

"Not anymore. He's been committed to a private mental institution in upstate New York," Piccolini said. He slumped down into the chair behind his desk and stared at Reardon, waiting.

Reardon was incredulous. "When?"

"This morning."

"Who told you?"

"What difference does it make?"

"I have a right to know," Reardon said. This case, he knew, had very nearly broken him. He had been taken off it and reinstated like a puppet jerked on and off a stage. He had pried open secret, hidden lives and left them spilled out in the light of day where they filled the air with pain. He had endangered his career and reputation, even his sanity. Because of that, because of all that, he had a right to know.

"Somebody downtown told me," Piccolini said.

Reardon looked at Piccolini accusingly. "You told them about the witness, about Mrs. Lassiter, about her making a positive ID of Dwight."

"So what?" Piccolini said. "They're my superiors. I don't run the New York City Police Department."

"You told the people downtown, and they told Wallace Van Allen," Reardon said. "And they just placed Dwight in a hospital. And that'll be the end of the case." He looked at Piccolini. "That *will* be the end of it, won't it? They'll just put a cap on it like a well with an embarrassing skeleton lying at the bottom of it. Karen Ortovsky's skeleton. Lee McDonald's skeleton."

"What difference does it make?" Piccolini said nervously.

Reardon shook his head with amazement. "Jesus Christ," he said. "They do have their own way of taking care of things, don't they?"

Piccolini shifted in his seat. He looked small, shriveled, as if the flame that burned in Reardon's eyes had singed and finally scorched him. "Like I said, what difference does it make? The kid is off the streets. The women he might or might not hurt are out of danger."

"For a while at least."

"For a long time," Piccolini said. "You can be sure of that."

"For as long as Wallace Van Allen wants him off the streets," Reardon said. "That's how long he's off the streets."

Piccolini waved Reardon's remark away with a sigh. "Anyway the women of New York are safer tonight," he said halfheartedly, and Reardon could see that Piccolini could not look him straight in the eye.

"Bullshit," Reardon said.

Piccolini ignored him. "And we don't have to worry about Petrakis."

"You have to release him. I got a positive ID of Dwight Van Allen," Reardon said. He could not believe what was going on around him.

Piccolini glanced furtively at Reardon. Then he said, almost in a whisper, "Petrakis' fingerprints were all over the ax."

"Release him!"

Piccolini leaned back wearily in his chair. "Jesus Christ," he said quietly, almost as if hoping Reardon would not hear him, "what the hell are we arguing about? I couldn't release him if I wanted to."

"What the hell is going on here?" Reardon said.

Piccolini's face turned serious. "You don't know?"

Reardon stared menacingly into Piccolini's face. "What is it?" he asked coldly.

Piccolini cleared his throat and looked Reardon straight in the eyes. "Petrakis killed himself. He slashed his wrists in the Tombs. Bled to death."

For a few spiraling seconds, Reardon could have sworn that the earth shifted under his feet. It was like that moment on the corner of Park Avenue when he had lost his bearings and had not known where he was.

But it was laced with a deeper sense of loss, a fundamental helplessness more awesome and devastating.

Reardon walked out of Piccolini's office and left the
station house. He kept on walking until the chill wind
seemed to scatter everything. And as he walked he
tried to gather in the loose ends of the case like wind-
blown strands of hair. He wanted to isolate what had
happened, know about it in some fundamental way. But
it was all too jumbled in his mind. All that he could
capture of it was a sense of its enormity and impenetrable complexity. Something about wealth and power
was here, and something about poverty and weakness,
but Reardon recognized that he did not have the means
to make sense of it.

And so he walked until afternoon became late afternoon, and late afternoon became night. He walked
through the city, but he knew that he no longer really
saw it. All those forms and structures and routines and
functions that once had given it a certain dreadful stability were dissolving. Everything seemed in the process of closing in, and yet, at the same time, suspended
precariously between chaos and absolute rigidity. Some
great engine had crushed Andros Petrakis, but Reardon
could not draw its image in his mind. Whatever it was,
he knew that no interrogation room could contain it.

Finally he sat down on a bench in the Children's
Zoo and gazed at the silent, empty cage of the fallow
deer. He was exhausted. He did not know what he
would do tomorrow, or the next day, or any day after
that.

After a while he rose and walked up the stairs to
Fifth Avenue. A sidewalk newsstand stood to his left
and he stopped to buy a newspaper, more as a gesture
of tribute to his father than anything else, remembering

how on that day long ago when he was still a child his father had defended the blind newsdealer, how he had struck out in the wild and hopeful gesture of a questioner of Cain.

Reardon pulled a ten-dollar bill from his wallet and placed it in the newsdealer's hand. *"Daily News,* please."

"A single, sir?" the newsdealer asked.

Only then did Reardon see that the man was blind. For a moment he stared at the white, sightless eyes and the slight palsied trembling of the hand that held the bill.

"Yes," he said, then, with an inexplicable feeling of resistance and renewal, "yes, it's a single."